"I like discoveri...
Dixie said

And Nick knew t... ...kinds of trouble. ... ...an at her cheek because ...g..e shouldn't and he really wanted the connection. "What makes Dixie Carmichael tick?" Nick asked.

"I can't resist poking my nose in where it doesn't belong. But I didn't realize I wanted to do it for a living till lately."

"Read one of those 'getting in tune with your inner self' books?"

"Woke up from a three-year coma that was a side effect of a messy divorce. I decided to get on with the business of living, doing what I really wanted because wallowing in self-pity wasn't getting me anywhere."

"Can't imagine you doing the pity routine. It's just not you. You're too..." *Feisty, energetic, fun.*

And he wanted so badly to kiss her he could almost taste her sweet lips on his.

Hi, Everyone!

Welcome back to Whistlers Bend. This is Dixie and Nick's story, two smart people who think they have the rest of their lives all figured out...until they cross paths in a little town in Montana and nothing is ever the same again.

The lump in Dixie's breast is benign and she knows she's gotten a second chance at life, to do what she's always wanted. She's giving up this one-horse town—or is that a one-buffalo town—to do the exciting, adventurous things she's always dreamed of. She's going to be a reporter in Denver.

Nick Romero is on his last undercover assignment as an FBI agent and has had enough excitement and adventure to last a lifetime. He wants to retire, settle down, open an Italian restaurant and fish. How can Dixie and Nick stay together when they're headed in opposite directions?

Take another trip with me and find out how Dixie and Nick work things out, if Maggie hunts down the right dress and marries Jack, how BJ and Flynn expand their family even more, how they catch the smugglers and if Andy is finally ready to come back home and fulfill his manly duties.

See you in Whistlers Bend for fun, sass and a whole lot of romance, and come visit me at www.DianneCastell.com.

Peeps to you!

Dianne

A FABULOUS WEDDING

Dianne Castell

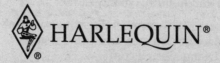

HARLEQUIN®

TORONTO • NEW YORK • LONDON
AMSTERDAM • PARIS • SYDNEY • HAMBURG
STOCKHOLM • ATHENS • TOKYO • MILAN • MADRID
PRAGUE • WARSAW • BUDAPEST • AUCKLAND

ISBN 0-373-75099-4

A FABULOUS WEDDING

Copyright © 2005 by Dianne Kruetzkamp.

www.eHarlequin.com

Printed in U.S.A.

To Gina. Always happy, always fun, a spirit of true joy.
You are the light of my life.

To the gals at the Snooty Fox, who know a real
Louis Vuitton from a knockoff in two seconds flat.
You're the best!

Books by Dianne Castell

HARLEQUIN AMERICAN ROMANCE

*Forty & Fabulous

Chapter One

Dixie twisted her fingers in the white sheet as she lay perfectly still on the examining table and tried to remember to breathe. Fear settled in her belly like sour milk. *She was scared!* Bone-numbing, jelly-legged, full-blown-migraine petrified. It wasn't every day that her left breast got turned into a giant pincushion.

She closed her eyes, not wanting to look at the ultrasound machine or think about the biopsy needle or anything else in the overly bright sterile room that would determine if *the lump* was really bad news.

She clenched her teeth so they wouldn't chatter, then prayed for herself and all women who had ever, or would ever, go through *this*. Waiting to find out was more terrifying than her divorce and wrapping her Camaro around a tree rolled into one.

God, let me out of this and I'll change. I swear it. No more pity parties over Danny's dumping her for that Victoria's Secret model, no more finding comfort in junk food, no more telling people how to live their lives and not really living her own. And if that meant leaving Whistlers Bend, she'd suck it up and do it and quit making excuses.

"We're taking out the fluid now," the surgeon said. "It's…"

Dixie's eyes shot wide open.

"It's clear."

Dixie swallowed, and finally got out, "Meaning?"

The surgeon's eyes stayed focused on what she was doing but they smiled, Dixie could tell. She'd developed the ability to read people from having waited tables at the Purple Sage Restaurant for three years and dealing with happy, sad and everything in between customers.

The surgeon continued. "Meaning the lump in your breast is a cyst. I'll send the fluid off to the pathologist to be certain, but the lump appears to be no more than a nuisance."

A nuisance! A nuisance was a telemarketer, a traffic ticket, gaining five pounds! Still, the important thing was—*she'd escaped*. She said another prayer for the women who wouldn't escape. She dressed, left the hospital and resisted the urge to turn handsprings all the way to her car. Or maybe she did turn handsprings—she wasn't sure.

She was on her way home. In one hour she'd be back in Whistlers Bend. Her life still belonged to her, and not to doctors and hospitals and pills and procedures. She fired up her Camaro and sat for a moment, appreciating the familiar idle of her favorite car as she stared out at the flat landscape of Billings, Montana. This was one of those definitive moments when life smacked her upside the head and said, *Dixie, old girl, get your ass in gear. You've wanted action, adventure, hair-raising experiences for as long as you can remember.*

Now's the time to make them happen!

"NICK ROMERO." He stood on the piece-of-junk ladder he'd found in the back room of the Curly Cactus and unscrewed the curtain rod with the electric-pink curtains that gave him an upset stomach just looking at them. The bracket let go, swung free, and the material slid off the rod onto the floor with the green rug straight from someone's garage sale.

Not that he understood the inner workings of garage sales. Twenty years in the FBI didn't lend itself to that unless the garage contained something stolen, smuggled, dead or held hostage, and the sale was guns, drugs, cars or even people.

But all that would soon be over. He was quitting the bureau and getting lost in some little town where no one would know he was ex-FBI. Anonymity would increase his chances for old age. He'd open a restaurant that really was his and not a front for an investigation like this one.

He'd had enough action to fill two lifetimes. It was the main reason he'd had a girlfriend, not a wife, who'd left him for a high-school history teacher. The FBI had been his life, till he'd woken up one morning and couldn't remember if he was in his apartment or on assignment because both places looked the same, and he was alone.

He wanted permanence in his life for a change. He wanted his primary concern to be perfecting an Alfredo sauce, the only thing fired his way compliments on his linguini, the biggest danger an overbaked casserole of Nonna Celest's ziti.

He dragged the ladder to the other side of the window and was undoing the other bracket when he heard "I'm too sexy for this town" coming from the back entrance. A woman in a denim skirt, scoop-necked green blouse and a cowboy hat in hand pranced into the room, oblivious to him on his ladder.

He jumped down, noticing great brown eyes, soft skin, a woman in her early forties, who smelled like heaven on earth, and had the most sensual mouth he'd ever seen.

"Who are you?" she asked. "What have you done with Jan?" She gazed around. "And what in the almighty world have you done to the Curly Cactus? It's…ruined."

Her eyes turned to slits and her lips thinned. "Is this one of those makeover shows? I hate makeover shows. The Curly Cactus doesn't need a makeover. It's perfect the way it is…was."

He folded his arms and gazed down at her. "Sorry you feel like that. I bought the place and—"

"*You're* going to run the Curly Cactus?" She wiggled her brows and gave him a critical once-over as she sashayed around him. "Well, you're handsome enough—I'll give you that. You'd probably get business on your looks alone. But I sure hope you're good at running a salon, or you won't last in this town. Women here take their hair real serious."

She faced the bank of mirrors and went on without taking a breath. "So, how about starting with me. I need a dye job. Make the red a little brighter. Mine is sort of drab auburn. I'm thinking Lucille Ball red. Some pizzazz."

Who the hell was this ball of fire? What had happened to laid-back, aw-shucks and moseying-and-meandering western? He'd been warned he'd have to change his big-city ways to fit in. But this woman wore him out just listening to her.

His cell phone rang, and he snatched it from the counter, checking the number. *Mother,* which translated into Wes Cutter, his contact and partner for the past ten years. "Hey, Mom," he greeted Wes, who just loved being called that. "I got company right now. Call you back." Nick disconnected and said to the gal with the delicious lips, "I'm not *running* the Curly Cactus."

"That wasn't a very nice way to talk to your mother. She raised you, you know. Cared for you when you were sick. You should call her back and apologize."

Okay, so this *was* the west. Small-town values, neighbors and where *mother* really did refer to the woman who'd given you life and wasn't a derogatory term men used with one another. He pointed at the swivel chairs, wash basins and dryers and tried for a good-old-boy stance. "I'm running a family restaurant. Moving all this stuff into the shed out back. Going to sell it on eBay."

The woman's brown eyes shot wide open. "No!"

"EBay's the best." Except maybe in rural America? "Or I'll sell it at a garage sale." See, he was getting the hang of this. That sounded more hometown, right?

"This is awful. Why would Jan sell?" The gal walked around. "I don't get it. She was happy here. Everybody was happy here—at least, the females. No matter how bad your day was you could come to Jan for a manicure and feel better, leave all your problems behind. This place is—*make that was*—great." She stared back at him, none too happy. "And now you've killed it."

How could anyone flip out over a salon? "Jan was tired of Montana winters and wanted sun. You can understand that." And the FBI had paid her a potful of money and thrown in a new car so they could move in ASAP to try to find some smugglers.

"You're really not opening a salon?"

He pointed to his chest. "I do calamari, not curls, lady."

"Lady? Maybe I should just call you *man*." The woman grabbed a handful of her hair. "What am I supposed to do with *this?* I need color." She wiggled her fingers at him. "I need my nails done. I need pampering. I've had a rough three days."

"Give me some time and I'll rustle you up some grub."

What she gave him was a you-have-lost-your-mind look. Guess he'd carried the John Wayne attitude a little to far. He didn't get small-town western for crap—until she held out her arms, pulling her silk blouse tight over voluptuous curves and he suddenly got western just fine. *Oh, boy!*

"I'm a size fourteen. Do I look like I need grub? I need new hair to go with my new Stetson. I want Jan back. Jan's the hair diva."

"Well, she's going to be the diva in Sun City, Arizona. Nick's should be open soon. You'll have to deal."

"Are you always such a smart aleck?"

"Sorry. I've been working my—" *ass off,* he almost said, then settled on "—working really hard since I took over the place."

At least that part was true. Sheriff Jack Dawson had contacted the FBI two weeks ago, and since then Nick had been on fast-forward to get his cover together, learn more than he ever wanted to know about illegal designer stuff and move to Whistlers Bend, Montana, before the smugglers relocated to another town. This was the best lead the FBI had on these guys yet.

The gal jammed her Stetson on her head and peered up at him. "And how long ago did you take over this place?"

"Two days. The moving van pulled up yesterday and got Jan's belongings from her apartment upstairs, and I moved mine in. Thought everyone in town knew. The name's Nick Romero."

"Well, there you have it. I leave for three days and the town goes right to pot."

She pointed at him, suddenly smiling big. "I got it—I got it! How about we find you another place to open your restaurant? There's a vacancy down by Little Fish Lake. A boat rental. Nice view, good place for a restaurant. Bet if I talked to Jan she'd reconsider and got herself back here."

She grabbed his hand, her warm fingers making him…light-headed? *He needed lunch, a beer.* The stress of dealing with this small-town stuff was killing him.

She pulled on him, saying, "Let me take you to the lake. Beartooth Mountains in the distance, little yellow flowers, blue skies that go on forever. This place smells like perm and nail polish and shampoo.

Who wants to eat in a place that smells like that? Gross."

She said something else about chemicals and makeup, but he wasn't too sure with her holding his hand. *Damn, what was going on with him?* Too many assignments? Too little sleep? Culture shock! Why couldn't the saloon guy have agreed to sell? Nick would have fit in there, no problem. Order a beer, serve a beer.

He took back his hand. "I appreciate your loyalty to Jan and this Cactus place, but things change, times change. I'll open the windows, and once I get all this junk cleaned out the odor will go, too."

"Junk?"

"I'll paint and refinish the hardwood floors, get new carpet and—"

"But—"

"It'll be fine," he said, putting his hands to her shoulders to make his point. *Who was he kidding?* He'd wanted to touch her, feel that blouse. He took in her sparkling eyes and sassy demeanor. "You should run an ad," he advised her. "Get someone else in town to open a beauty shop. Maybe down by that lake."

"You're not comprehending this, are you? Jan is irreplaceable, especially with a restaurant named…"

"Nick's Place," he informed her as her fresh scent filled his head.

"Couldn't you at least call it something with a little more zing?"

"Like, the Curly Cactus was such a great name? What the hell's a curly cactus? Come around in a week or so. I'm a decent cook."

"I'm giving up food. I want Jan."

He folded his arms. "Then there's a road trip to Arizona in your future."

"Where are you from?"

"Denver." He'd never been to Denver, but he sure as hell had been to every other big city in the U.S.

"Well, Denver, I'd like to say welcome to Whistlers Bend, but my heart just isn't in it, and every woman in town's going to feel the same. I'd consider moving to the lake if I were you. No one's ever going to think of this place as a restaurant. Everyone'll blame you for chasing Jan away."

Fortunately, Jack Dawson pushed open the front door at that moment and strolled in, carrying a bag of groceries. Dixie pointed at Nick. "Arrest that man for…trespassing, disturbing the peace, anything you can think of. This is a beauty salon, for Pete's sake."

Jack pushed his Stetson to the back of his head and grinned. "I believe he's got a bill of sale, Dixie, and now he even has groceries." Jack set the bag on the counter and added, "Besides, you like Italian food."

"I can buy a pizza at the grocery. I can't buy new hair. What am I supposed to do? What are all the women in town supposed to do? This isn't over!" She tossed her head and pranced out the way she'd come, except this time mumbling instead of singing.

Something about her attracted him. She was… alive. Energetic and fresh. All the things he'd lost a long, long time ago.

Jack craned his neck around, checking to make sure the gal had left, then said, "I see you're settling in okay and have met some of the local color."

"Who *is* she?" Nick asked, trying to sound normally curious, but not feeling normal at all. Hell, normal for him was gun drawn as he yelled *FBI*.

"Dixie Carmichael. The go-to gal for news and gossip around here. She's also the one who saw the smugglers. They ate at the Purple Sage, the diner where she works, asking about the boy who found that fake Louis Vuitton wallet I called the FBI about. She knew something was up and phoned me, but by the time I arrived they'd gone."

"Which means she can ID them and they can return the favor. Where's the little boy?"

"On vacation for the summer with his grandmother. We got him out of town. I warned Dixie to be careful, but I don't think she took me seriously. She's kind of spirited."

Jack sat in one of the white swivel chairs and leaned back as he gazed out the window. "Can't believe we have smugglers in Whistlers Bend. Thought

I'd left that high-profile crap behind when I gave up the Chicago PD and moved here."

"It's the location. Rural, mountains, right in the middle of a bunch of expressways. The knockoff designer goods are made in the East, shipped here, then trucked inland. This is a great place to hide and transfer merchandise from bigger trucks to smaller ones for distribution."

"And you're here to find the trucks, persuade the drivers to roll over on the suppliers, then find the point of entry and confiscate the goods."

"Maybe get the foreign governments to stop the pirating. Luggage, perfumes, jewelry, shoes, you name it. I brought samples of the fakes so I'd know what the hell we're looking for. Three babies nearly died from contaminated jars of designer baby food last month. We've got to shut these bastards down and keep an eye on Dixie. I doubt if she has any idea what she's walked into. Knockoffs are big business. Billions."

"Be careful you don't blow your cover. She's got a knack for sticking her nose into everything around here."

Nick stroked his chin. "Hell, all that gal's interested in is having her hair dyed. I've been doing this FBI gig for twenty years, Jack. Dixie Carmichael's a piece of cake."

Jack laughed. "That's what I thought about Maggie when I got here from Chicago. Hold on to your butt, city boy. You're in for a rougher ride than you think."

HOW COULD JAN just up and leave! Dixie grumbled as she tromped toward the Purple Sage, past Pretty in Pink and the hardware store. She tried to picture the woman who'd done her hair for ten years, but instead that Nick guy she'd run into came to mind.

She gave herself a shake. She had no time or desire to get involved with any man, even if he did have great black hair and eyes and one dynamite build, and was a whole lot more exciting to look at than Jan ever was. Dixie Carmichael had an agenda. She had dreams to fulfill, dreams too long put off.

She pushed open the purple door to the Sage and made her way around the partially filled tables with purple Formica tops, past the counter with the doughnuts and a cherry pie winking at her from under a glass dome.

She ignored them—no more junk food, she'd promised herself—went to the usual table by the window and plopped down. Maggie, best friend number one, flipped through a wedding magazine. "Don't these editors think forty-year-olds get married? I need sleeves."

"And I need the Curly Cactus. What the heck happened to the place? I can't believe you let Jan go."

Maggie took a sip of tea. "You know, it was the craziest thing. One day Jan was here. The next she up and flew the coop. Went to live with her sister, I heard. We're trying to get Patti Jacobs to open a shop."

Dixie snapped the magazine shut to get Maggie's attention. "Patti grooms dogs. Sheers sheep. I'm not getting a good picture here." She thumped her hat. "Under this Stetson I have roots—big fat ones. We should boycott that Nick guy, get Jan to come back. Do whatever it takes."

Maggie opened the magazine again. "Well, the boycotting idea is not going to happen. See this guy?" She jabbed her finger at a gorgeous groom in the magazine. "He's good-looking, but he doesn't hold a candle to that Italian stallion down the street. He's single, and every woman in a fifty-mile radius is salivating and no one intends to boycott him. More like beat a path to his door. They're taking bets over at the Cut Loose on who's going to date him first. Pot's up to five hundred bucks."

"Boy, could I really use five hundred bucks," Dixie said as Dr. Barbara Jean Fairmont, who'd recently become MacIntire, drew up to the table.

She braced her arms, leaned over and glared at Dixie. "You told us you were going to Billings to see your accountant. I just got a fax from Billings Memorial. Billings Memorial's a real strange name for an accounting firm. I'm listed as your primary-care physician so they sent me your latest medical information." She parked in the chair beside Dixie and whispered, "They sent your biopsy results."

Maggie dropped her cup of tea onto her saucer with a clatter that drew stares. She paled. "Oh, no."

Dixie grinned. The best defense was a good offence, or something like that. "And I'm fine." She took BJ's hand. "The AMA frowns on doctors, especially pregnant ones, rendering bodily harm to their patients. I didn't want to worry either of you. One's on the nest. One's planning a wedding. Besides—" she did the big smiley-face thing "—I'm okay. Better than okay. I've got a new job."

"Don't try to change the subject," BJ huffed. "I'm still furious with you. I'm beyond furious. I'm pissed as hell!"

Maggie gasped. "You're leaving the Sage?"

"I'm a reporter for the *Whistle Stop*," Dixie said. "Isn't that great? But I'm not leaving here. The Sage is where I'll find out what to report on. More gossip is tossed across these tables than fried eggs and ham. I always wanted to go to the city and work on a big paper. My plan is to scoop some story here that'll be great on my résumé."

Maggie and BJ exchanged glances and Maggie finally managed in a weak voice, "You're leaving us, as in going somewhere else? What will we do? We've met at this table for thirteen years, ever since I moved back from Chicago after divorcing Jack."

"And now you're marrying him again and BJ has Flynn and the kids. I need something, too. I want adventure, excitement, trouble. You know how I love trouble. I get all twitterpaited just thinking about trouble. You both went away—medical school, art school. I married Danny the dope right out community college. I now live with my sister and her two kids, in a house a block from where I grew up. My big vacation each year is visiting my folks in Tampa. I want a real life before it's too late."

Maggie leveled her a hard look. "Except I got a bad feeling about this story you're going after. It's that knockoff wallet situation, isn't it? And the guys who came after Drew because he saw them. I'm right, aren't I?"

Without giving Dixie a chance to contrive a good excuse, Maggie added, "Are you out of your flipping mind?"

BJ pursed her lips. "I've got a better idea, one that's much more fun. Go after that Nick person who's opening the restaurant, instead. That's an adventure. Men are always an adventure." She grinned and patted her still flat stomach, which wouldn't be flat much longer. "I speak from experience. That guy's handsome and very well-built. Much more interesting than a wallet, and a whole lot safer… maybe."

"But I don't want safe. And I definitely don't want a man, especially a boring cook, no matter how attractive he is." She smiled. "Except I sure could use the five hundred dollars."

"Meaning you're going to give him a tumble?" BJ asked.

"Meaning I'm going to get a date with him and collect the money, and then run like hell."

THE NOON SUN blazed overhead as Nick pushed the dolly holding the last white salon swivel chair down the stone walk toward the shed behind the restaurant. Not that he had to accomplish all that much while here; he just had to give the impression of working to fix the place up. This was a *front,* after all. He had to look as though he was getting ready to open a restaurant, while really tracking down the smugglers.

Oh, he'd concoct some of his grandmother's— Nonna Celest's—recipes and let heavenly smells waft through town and drive everyone nuts. But as soon as this caper was over, he was out of here to start anew. He'd read, fish, be bored. Buy a house and mow grass. That was what ordinary people did and he just wanted to be ordinary.

Now was a good time to practice fitting in and being one of the townfolk. The more people accepted him as just a guy, the more they'd open up. Someone had to have seen the trucks or strangers showing up from time to time. Anything could lead him to nailing the smugglers. He'd learned long ago that the smallest detail could be the biggest clue.

He dragged the salon chair into the shed and parked it beside the other two chairs and wash basins he'd hauled in earlier. When he came out, Dixie Carmichael was strolling toward him, carrying a basket and waving as though she'd known him all her life. What had happened to make her so friendly today after she'd wanted him to drop off the earth yesterday? She was after something, no doubt.

She had a blue bandana on her head, little tufts of red frizz sticking out at the sides. "See you got curls without Jan around to help."

"This?" She plucked a section of hair that resembled one of those copper-colored metal scouring pads. A spark of…was that murder?…showed in her eyes for a second. But then she smiled sweetly, a little too sweetly, and said, "Had to take matters into my own hands. Gave myself a dye-and-perm job. Except I mixed up the times. Doubled the time I left on the perm solution and halved the dye time. I figured it would all work out in the end. It didn't. This is the fried Chia Pet look."

He suppressed a laugh. Never, ever laugh at a woman's hair, no matter what. Being over forty, he was old enough and wise enough to know that. "Dye it back the way it was."

"If I do anything else to my hair using chemicals there's a good chance all the ends will break and I'll have paintbrush stubs." She swung her basket. "But I didn't come here to talk hair. I came to welcome you to Whistlers Bend and the surrounding territory. What about taking a holiday from renovations-by-Nick and joining me on a picnic? It's a beautiful day and I can show you the area, point out places of interest, be your own personal tour guide. What a deal, right?"

Ah, the small-town ways. This was the third picnic he'd been invited on since he'd gotten here. He'd begged off the others, needing a few days to get the feel of the place and the people, and he should do the same now. Still, he had to fit in. Turning down invitations was not fitting in. But why was Dixie asking him out now, when she'd wanted him gone before? "Does this mean you've forgiven me for taking over the Curly Cactus?"

Her eyes crossed and her face reddened, but she recovered and then managed a cheery tone and said, "Forgiven? Why, of course I've forgiven you. That's the reason I'm here. And to make you feel welcome."

Something was up, and it wasn't her love of picnics or of him. "Mary Lou Armstrong, a teller at the bank, said she'd stop by later on."

Not that he wanted to see Mary Lou, but she probably knew the workings at the bank, if someone was suddenly getting rich, could be a snitch for the smugglers. Besides, he wanted to see Dixie's reaction. What was she after?

"Mary Lou?" Dixie's smile froze. "How nice." She yanked back the cover of her basket. "Fried chicken and blueberry pie. Surely anything Mary Lou has in mind can wait. Bet you're hungry. Thought we'd head up to the old depot and abandoned silver mine. It would give you some history of the place and you could look around. We could mix business and pleasure. One of the kids found a knockoff wallet there. That's a wallet that's supposed to be by a designer but is really a fake. There might be some illegal activity in the area, and I thought I'd poke around for a story. I'm working part-time as a reporter for the *Whistle Stop*."

The hair on his arms stood straight up. What the hell did she think she was doing, poking around in something so dangerous? Any story she got might well end up as her obituary. The smugglers were out there and knew what she looked like, and they'd put a stop to some cub reporter on a two-bit newspaper getting into their business.

Dixie Carmichael was beautiful, tenacious and feisty as hell, and she was walking into one giant mess.

Chapter Two

But Nick couldn't say any of that to Dixie or he'd blow his cover sky-high. He slipped into good-old-boy mode. "Poking around in something like this sounds dangerous. Don't know if I'd be doing that if I were you. Leave it to the sheriff. He seemed like a pretty competent guy."

She gave him a devilish grin. "But I have a plan. If I can break this story it'll be huge and I can nail a job on a city newspaper, something I've always wanted to do. You're from Denver. Know anyone at the *Denver Post?* Maybe you can put in a word for me."

"Maybe you should report on something else." *Like what? What happened in small towns?* "Quilting," he offered. "It's really coming into its own these days. And baking. Bet you do great pies."

"No big-city newspaper is going to pick me up because I write a story on baking a pie. I need something juicy. Something people can relate to. Everyone's heard about knockoffs, been tempted to buy one at some time. This story will drive home where those bogus items come from and how buying them supports activities people hate most."

"If you don't get killed first!" Damn, how'd that slipped out? Because she was putting herself right in harm's way.

She gave him a patronizing smile. "I'm not trying to be a one-woman vigilante committee. I know the territory. I'll be fine. Besides, I have an advantage. No one thinks a forty-year-old full-figured woman like me would snoop into smuggling. My appearance puts people at ease. That's the trouble with those *Alias* women on TV. They look like badasses and get themselves into trouble every time. I look like a…soccer mom." She patted the bandana. "I have a built-in cover."

Well, she definitely had the *built* part down! *Focus, Nick, focus, and not on Dixie's breasts.* He should stay away from her and keep his mind on the job. Except, Dixie was the job. With or without him, she'd trot off to search for evidence or clues on the smuggling case. He couldn't let her go off alone and if he got Jack to go with her, she'd know Nick had informed the sheriff and she might start wondering why Jack and the new chef in town were so close. He had to keep his cover. He had to go.

"You know, I should check out some of the

streams and lakes for trout. I have a fresh-trout recipe that'll knock your socks off."

"Great." She smiled, and this time as though she
meant it. For a second he couldn't move. Her smile
was...*intoxicating*. Mesmerizing.

She added, "Write Mary Lou a little note that
you'll see her later."

"Mary Lou?"

Her brow furrowed. "Uh, the gal you're supposed
to meet. You can see her at the Cut Loose tonight."
Dixie gave a slight sway of her nicely rounded hips.
"Since I'm taking you up to the caves and showing
you the streams, you can buy me a beer later. It'll be
fun. I'll teach you the Montana two-step."

"Sure." He had no idea what the hell he'd just
agreed to; all he could think about was her hips.
Great hips. Womanly hips. "You bet."

She grinned. "Then we have a date for tonight.
You and me, right?"

AND THE *five hundred dollars will be all mine,* Dixie
thought. She nodded toward the restaurant. "Tape a
note for Mary Lou to the front door. She'll get the
message."

The message being, Dixie Carmichael landed the
new fish on the block and you didn't. "We'll take my
car. I know the roads. I'll wait out front. I'm parked
on the street."

He gave her a quick nod, then made for the back door. He seemed a little off balance. Probably working too hard. She retraced her steps around the old redbrick building. Nick Romero was a strange guy. He looked rugged enough, as Maggie had said, but he wasn't at all. Yesterday he'd been a little rough around the edges, probably from the fatigue of moving in and setting things up, but he wasn't that way today.

He didn't think much of snooping or taking chances of any sort. He liked articles about baking and quilting. Then again, he was a chef, and they weren't known for daring and risk-taking unless they had a pan and stove in front of them.

She smiled to herself as she put the picnic basket in the Camaro. She liked his being more laid-back and not one of those testosterone-driven kind of guys. Maggie had Jack, her Chicago cop, now local sheriff and soon-to-be husband. BJ had Colonel Flynn MacIntire, local war hero and U.S. Army poster man, a true hero on all fronts. Danny boy, her own rat-fink ex, was a Donald Trump clone who always had a business deal going on. A mild-mannered chef was a nice change of pace, even for an afternoon picnic and one-time trip to the Cut Loose to win a bet.

A warm summer breeze stirred down the main drag of Whistlers Bend, gusting through the pines and oaks that lined the street, flapping the purple awning on the Sage. She watched the Montana-blue sky, stretching on forever except for the hint of clouds in the distance. Nick might need a jacket. Storms blew up in the mountains without much warning.

She skipped up the few steps to the Curly Cactus. The front door was slightly ajar. Jan had always had a hard time getting it to latch. Dixie walked in, intending to yell for Nick, but she stopped dead. He was talking to someone in the hallway, a phone conversation. He told the caller he had to go because he was going on a picnic to fit in around here, and that the caller should stop over later so they could figure out what to do about their current situation.

Was Nick speaking to Mary Lou? It wasn't an airhead Mary Lou kind of chat, more a guy-to-guy exchange. Did Nick know anyone that well in town? It had to be in town or nearby if the caller was stopping over. The polite thing for Dixie to do was to make her presence known, except…except something felt off and good manners got outdone by basic curiosity.

Her left eye twitched, and it hadn't done that in three years, since Danny had gone away on that Cancún business trip, then asked for a divorce.

Quietly, Dixie backed out of the room, leaving the door as she'd found it. She sprinted for the Camaro, jumped inside and slapped a smile on her face, hoping for the innocent look—as if minding her own business, twiddling her thumbs, just waiting for her date.

Nick strolled out the front door, smiled, waved,

taped the note to the door, then came her way. As he climbed into the car, she asked in a sweet little voice, "Everything all right?"

"Sorry I was so long. Didn't know what to say to Mary Lou in the note and I got a call from Mother."

That was so not a mother conversation. Why would Nick lie? What was going on with the handsome, laid-back and very mysterious man from Denver? Only one way to find out: pump him for info and hope he'd let something slip.

"Did you happen to see anyone come in while you were out here? Thought I heard someone in the house."

She gulped, then grinned. She wasn't as good at this snooping thing as she'd thought. "Not a soul. Must have been the wind blowing through the place." She nodded at the horizon. "We'll probably have some rain blowing in tonight. Good thing you brought a jacket."

She fired the engine and quickly added so that he couldn't ask her more questions, "So, how'd you get to be such a great cook and want to open your own place? Culinary school? Prestigious internships at five-star restaurants? And what brings you to Whistlers Bend? Kind of far from Denver. Does your mother live there?"

He gave her a sideways glance.

Uh-oh! Too many questions at one time. Pump-

ing for info was not drilling for it! She needed to re-
coup, offer something of her own so he'd feel comfortable and give something in return. She smiled,
then he smiled, and she nearly swerved into Pretty
and Pink.

"Hey," he said, grabbing for the wheel. "Careful."

And that was exactly what she had to be—
careful. Nick Romero was some kind of man. So
gorgeous, a smile to die for, and this time she almost
had—literally. His breath warmed her cheek, and his
large hands holding hers felt…*good*. Really good!
This was not part of being a snoop.

"You okay?" he asked.

She gripped the wheel tighter and focused on the
road heading out of town and not on Nick so near.
"My parents moved to Florida. They love the warm
weather and ocean. Ever been there?"

"Excuse me?" She glanced at him out of the corner of her eye. He had a confused look on his face.
"You want to pull over for a minute?"

"I'm fine. Terrific." *Sort of, if she could quit ob-
sessing over Nick Romero.* Except, he smelled really
delicious and had wavy hair she wanted to touch. No
touching! "Tell me about your life as a chef."

"You sure you don't want to get a drink or
something?"

"How'd you wind up in Whistlers Bend?"

Nick sat back in his seat. "A friend of mine came

through here last year on his way to Glacier National Park. Knowing how I wanted to open my own place in a small town, he suggested I contact merchants to see if anyone wanted to sell. He said Whistlers Bend had nice people, needed a restaurant. Seemed like a good match for me."

"Guess I did hear something about that. But we already have the Purple Sage."

"It's a diner. Now you'll have Nick's, and folks won't have to travel to Billings for dinner."

She aimed the car onto a gravel road and they dropped into a pothole that threatened to swallow her front tire. "This road isn't made for my Camaro. I'll have to go slow."

Nick held on to the dashboard as the car bounced from pothole to pothole. "Is this the only way to the mine?"

She eased the car forward. "Quickest way from town, but there are other roads to the west that come in along the base of the mountains. They're closer to the expressways and in better shape."

This was good. They were two people talking, and Nick was just a guy. Was that like saying a Humvee was just a car? "I think the roads are the reason the smugglers meet around here. They rendezvous in different places, split up the goods from bigger trucks that drive in from the west coast, then get back on the expressways and take the stuff to the cities. The switch would take minutes and they'd be on their way. In the winter they probably move the operation south because the mountain roads up here would be impossible."

He didn't respond for a moment. "How…how'd you think of that?"

She shrugged. "A hunch. There's got to be some reason the smugglers are hiding out here. Whistlers Bend's proximity to the expressways is something to consider. Heck, if I were a smuggler, remote and accessible to expressways is what I'd look for. And we have the infamous found wallet, big truck sightings, plus nasty guys asking about a little boy. Not usual Whistlers Bend happenings. I think little old Whistlers Bend is smack-dab in the middle of the smuggling ring."

He laughed. "You have a great imagination. Maybe you should write fiction." Nick cinched in his seat belt as another pothole threatened to put his head against the roof. "This is some road."

"Once in a while the high schoolers drive up to drag race. The road levels out by the depot, but even that's pretty grown over. I've heard there are shallow caves around the side. No action up here at night. Road's too bad, and without light it's easy to drive into a ditch."

"So what exactly are we…I mean you…looking for?"

"Good question." She dodged a rock that had washed onto the road and pointed out the window to another rutted road. "A mile or so down the way is a good stream for trout, with a lake beyond. Best spot is over the old railroad tracks under the big pines. We have deer, racoons, bears, the usual."

She might not fish for trout, but that didn't mean she didn't fish for other things. "Maybe you can borrow Jack's truck and find your way up? You two are friendly." She glanced at him, gave him a quick look to get his reaction about knowing Jack. Nothing but a blank face.

"Just met him yesterday when you came in. Tell me about the old mine."

Except, he and Jack acted as though they knew each other, and Jack seemed…tense about something. Nick Romero got curiouser and curiouser. Especially since his inquiry felt more like a reason to change subjects than genuine interest.

"When the mine ran full tilt, the trains took away the silver. Sounded their whistles as they rounded the bend to warn the miners to get off the tracks. A town grew up to provide supplies and ranching caught on. When the mine petered out, the town survived."

She pointed ahead. "There's the old train depot, or what's left of it. We can eat on the porch and you can tell me all about yourself." Did that sound nonchalant enough? Like two people on a picnic, talking to pass the time?

"Not much left to tell."

Right! "Everyone's got a story. Everyone keeps secrets."

He shrugged and gazed into the distance. "Not boring cooks from Denver who move to Montana to dish up manicotti and lasagna."

DAMN, DIXIE CARMICHAEL was one inquisitive woman. And smart! How'd she put together all that smuggling stuff? Her hunch was right on the money! She was a real reporter. Nose in everywhere it didn't belong, driving law enforcement nuts, putting herself in the middle of a dangerous situation for a story!

And even worse…she smelled of vanilla and sunshine, and had a hint of devilment in her eyes. She made him…edgy, dammit, and after all those years with the bureau and on more cases than he could count, that was saying one hell of a lot. He had to get a lead on these smugglers, close them down, make sure Dixie was safe, then get the hell out of Dodge… or in this case, Whistlers Bend…and get on with his quiet life.

She pulled the Camaro next to the depot and killed the engine. Silence fell around them as he got out and took in his surroundings. They were so alone he might as well be on Mars, except that Mars had never looked like this. "This sky—it's so…"

"Blue?" She stuck her elbow out the open window and rested her chin on her arm as she gazed at him. She appeared to like what she saw, and he sure as hell liked looking at her.

"And big." He swiped his forehead. "It's starting to bake out here. Is August always like this? Thought it would be getting colder."

"The nights are, and in another two weeks summer will give way to autumn. The aspen turn gold and the Canada geese take off south, honking their way across the sky." Dixie stepped from the car and snagged the basket and blanket from the back, along with a baseball cap. She handed the cap to him. "Not exactly a Stetson, but it'll keep the sun out of your eyes."

He took the navy blue hat. "What's with *Hope* written under the bill? New fad? Put the logo under the brim instead of on top?"

She walked to the depot. Insects buzzed; the wind swished through the weeds. "To support women with breast cancer. *Hope*'s written underneath because breast cancer makes a woman's life upside down. I'm thinking about setting up a 5-K run-walk-stroll-whatever in the Bend. Make folks more aware, hand out literature, raise money for research."

He slipped the hat on. "I'll handle the food."

She stopped, making him stop, too. Her eyebrows drew together. "That's a huge job."

He shrugged. "My grandmother's a breast cancer

survivor. She had a mastectomy ten years ago. Scared the hell out of me." He gave Dixie a quick nod. "I've done this before, in...Denver. Pizza works well with a crowd. My mushroom pizza is the best. Old family recipe."

"Where's your grandmother now?"

"Living in Italy with her new husband." Nick grinned. "Alonzo is a great guy."

Dixie bumped against him on purpose, one of those friendly bumps between two people who share something unique. "Good for grandmother." Dixie peered up at him. "You surprise the heck out of me, Nick Romero. I think I have you pegged and then I don't. You're a man of mystery." She flashed the smile that made his toes curl and drove the air right out of his lungs.

She wasn't just a beautiful snoop: she was a compassionate, understanding, proactive beautiful snoop. The kind that could suck him right in. Holy crap!

"Something wrong?"

Hell, yes! He was attracted to her more and more. "Nope, not a thing."

Dammit all! He had to get his mind off Dixie. Being distracted could too easily end with him and her on a cold, stainless-steel slab with tags on their big toes. "Hey, I'm starved. Can't wait to get to that chicken. Just smelling it drove me crazy all the way up here."

He snapped the basket from her hand and stepped onto the porch, the rotting boards sagging under his weight, the drooping roof blocking out the sun.

This was good. Keep things light, fun, not personal. No more reasons to like her. Heaven knows he had enough already. He continued. "You realize there aren't going to be any clues around here. This place is too out in the open for smugglers. I'm not the sheriff, but I can't see smugglers meeting here. Too risky. Doesn't make sense. We should eat and go."

She fluffed the blanket out and they sat down as he went on. "Give up the smugglers and concentrate on the 5-K event. That could be a really fine story."

She popped open containers of chicken and potato salad and handed him a plate. "The smugglers were here, Nick. Not here as by the depot, but by the mine." She picked up a chicken leg and pointed it at the side of a mountain. "The cave where Drew found the wallet is behind those trees. Great place to park a truck and hide out till whatever or whoever you're waiting for shows up."

"You've been watching too much *CSI*." He sank his teeth into the terrific fried chicken. "Oh, this is incredible. Give me the recipe."

"Takeout at the Purple Sage."

"Then I've got some serious competition." He wolfed down the chicken and started on the potato salad. A hawk circled overhead; another breeze rolled across the porch. "It's like we're the only two people on earth up here. How can you give this up for a city?" He aimed for small talk, and suddenly realized he truly liked it here. "This place is great, Dixie. It's near perfect."

"Being a reporter is something I have to do." She wiped her hands on a napkin and passed him an apple. "Let's check out the mine."

He held up a forkful of potato salad and said around a mouthful, "Hey, I'm not finished eating."

"Rain's coming in." She nodded at the horizon. "I dread facing that road in my Camaro if we get a downpour."

Rain was good. Put an end to their time and he'd get back here tomorrow alone and search around without her. "We should leave now to avoid the storm."

She gave him a long, thoughtful look. "You don't like this snooping around at all, do you?"

You have no idea is what he thought, then said, "It's a waste of time, since you have a capable sheriff. You can ask him for any information he finds and get your story that way."

She pursed her lips…her very kissable lips. "Jack's a great sheriff, but if he finds something he's sure not going to share it with me. He'll go running to the FBI. Some guy in a blue suit will fumble his way around here because he's unfamiliar with the territory, tip off the big newspapers, and there goes my chance at a scoop. The plans for my dream and the rest of my life go right down the drain."

She snapped the lids back on the food, leaving him with the apple and a drumstick. "But I'm hungry."

She stood and winked at him. He nearly swallowed the drumstick whole. "You're a cook. Deal. Let's get going. We're running out of time, and we can't have the rain washing away any clues that might be around."

Slowly, Nick got up, dusted off his hands and stretched, trying to waste time. He needed to get her away from the old depot and possibly finding clues that could involve her in the smuggling case, leading her right into more danger.

"Good grief. Get a move on," Dixie said as she grabbed his hand and pulled him toward trees and shrubs at the foot of the mountain. He stumbled after her. She might be only five-three, but there was nothing weak about Dixie Carmichael once she made up her mind.

Blue sky faded to gray, and she led him into the thicket of pines and weeds, where it was darker still. Dried needles formed a crunchy carpet; long thin pinecones lay here and there. "Storm's rolling in faster than I thought." She stopped for a minute. "Listen." She smiled as a strong gust blew around them. "I love the wind whistling in the pines. It's like God talking. You'll have to drive up here after a snowfall. It's so beautiful, spiritual. An out-of-body experience."

"Ever consider that God might be saying right now for us to get the hell out of here, that it's not safe?"

She yanked him on. "Nah, God wouldn't say *hell*. Besides, nothing's going to happen. It's broad daylight."

Nick wondered how many times that line had been uttered just before all hell broke loose.

They emerged from the cluster of trees and shrubs, facing a wall of rocks, low brush and bare ground. She pointed left. "Cave's that way. The mine's around the bend we just walked from."

"Okay, Lewis and Clark, then why'd we tramp our way through the trees?"

"Drew found the wallet around here somewhere and I want to cover all the bases. I'm sure Jack and his deputy, Roy, canvassed the area, but there's always a wind kicking up, blowing who knows what where. See if you find anything suspicious. I got a feeling…"

"What was Drew doing up here? Making out with his girlfriend?"

Dixie laughed while walking and searching, staring at the ground. "Drew's seven, and he was running away because he thought no one wanted him. Then BJ and Flynn adopted him and his brother, Petey.

Cute kids. A handful, since Petey has diabetes and Drew's hell on wheels. Now BJ's pregnant. She's also the town doctor. She'll have to get some help or clone herself."

Nick kicked at a pile of leaves to unearth anything trapped in them. "Where I'm from, runaway kids wind up in foster care or live on the street." *Unless they have a sainted grandmother to save their ass.*

She stopped and stared at him wide-eyed. "Denver's like that?"

Ah, hell! What a slip-up. This was supposed to be an easy cover for him, but when he was with Dixie, he let his guard down. Spending time close to the earth—in the earth, if they did the caves—got to him. "Just some parts of Denver. The tougher parts."

Did Denver have tougher parts? He had no idea. He'd never been. Now, Detroit…he knew all about growing up in the inner city. Till Nonna Celest—his Italian guardian angel who cooked like a dream, managed her own decorating business and sent him to a private school run like bootcamp—all but kidnapped him from his drunken mother and dragged him to Boston's north end. Grandma probably paid off his mother so she could adopt him outright—at least, that was what he'd always suspected. That sounded like Celest; certainly sounded like his mother! How could two women in the same family be so different?

Enough! He held Dixie's hand because he suddenly wanted—needed—a connection to someone he cared about. He did care about Dixie, and not just her hair and eyes and sexy ways. She was a good person; he could tell. He'd sure as hell met enough of the not-so-good types in his life.

"I see the entrance up ahead," he said. "We should investigate." Not that he wanted to right now, but he didn't want to answer any more freaking questions that could get him into trouble or send him back down Memory Lane.

"Wait," Dixie said as she pointed to a thorny-looking bush. She took her hand from his, pulled back a prickly branch and gingerly reached into the middle. She plucked out a piece of white paper he hadn't even noticed.

She held it up and he said, "A postcard?"

She studied it. "It's from Kate Spade."

"I'm thinking that's not a person in town, right?" He knew who Kate Spade was from the hours of instruction that representatives from that designer and others had drummed into his head. But most men *didn't* know squat about that stuff and he had to sound like a regular guy.

"Kate Spade is a designer for purses, wallets, clothes and the like. This is the card you'd find inside a purse or piece of luggage or whatever to register it with the company. But this one's for a knockoff. Look here." She pointed to the printing. "The last line is smudged. Designers who charge two-hundred-plus dollars for a purse do not smudge their registration cards. I learned that from BJ's mother. She's a whiz at knockoffs because she buys the real deal."

He slipped the card from her fingers and studied it. "Damn, you have good eyes. I didn't even see it." And that part was the truth.

She rolled her shoulders. "I'm shorter. I get a different angle from down here." Then she did a little dance, totally happy now and making him happy just watching her. "This is so great, Nick. I'm onto something big—I can feel it. Yee-haa!"

"Hey, it's only a card." He had to calm her down, discourage her so she wouldn't return. *Yeah, like that was going to happen!*

"The wallet and card didn't just fall out of the sky. This is huge, Nick. It really is."

She laughed again, the sound pure joy. "I love being a reporter."

Chapter Three

Oh, great, Nick thought. Dixie in a state of reporter euphoria was not what he wanted at all. Then she turned and threw her arms around his neck, surprising the hell out of him. Now, this he did want, even if he shouldn't.

Her chest touched his; her eyes sparkled with excitement, then suddenly sparkled with something more. They darkened to amber, then antique gold. She looked happy, so innocent, so damn pretty. He didn't need happy, innocent or pretty, but here they were, in one fascinating, dazzling woman who set him right on his ear in the middle of the mountains.

He slipped the bandana from her head, letting her hair fly free, the curls twirling in the wind, doing whatever they pleased. He stroked her cheek—smooth, silky, warm and inviting, so damn alluring.

She smiled, her eyes dreamy now as she stood on tiptoes, her lips parting to meet his, her breathing faster as he lowered his head, ready to taste her sweet mouth. Then a gust of wind hit, as if saying, *What the hell are you doing, Nick Romero?*

Holy crap, what was he doing? This was a job. He was lying to her at every turn, and there would never be anything between them because when she found out who he was, she'd wring his neck. Women didn't think much of men who used them, then walked away. He was using her to get information. Damn, he hated doing that, but he sure couldn't tell a reporter he was FBI on a case and expect her to keep it a secret.

Reporters didn't keep secrets for long. They blabbed and they even put them in print. No way could Dixie find out who he was or what he was up to.

He swallowed. Keeping his brain on the job and his eyes on her, as he stealthily slipped the card into his front pants pocket, then unwound her arms from his neck. He took a step back, every cell of his body protesting, wanting Dixie more and more. "I…I can't do this, Dixie." *He needed a reason, though, dammit!* Why wouldn't any man want to kiss Dixie Carmichael? "I'm not ready to…for…*this*."

What a crock! He was so ready he could barely think.

"It's just a kiss, Nick."

Her lips came a breath closer, her breasts pressing against his chest. He could feel the heat from her body making him hotter than he thought possible. Another gust hit, swaying the tress around them and swirling the undergrowth and leaves into a frenzy.

"We need to get out of here." If they didn't, he'd start something he couldn't finish without messing this assignment up big-time.

He scooped the bandana from the ground, then took her hand and led her back through the stand of pines before she could protest. Her fingers entwined with his. They felt good there, like they belonged. Connected. Except, getting together with Dixie was just part of the job, he had to remember *that!*

The storm was a stroke of good fortune. They'd leave before she unearthed something else. Dixie truly did have a knack for finding stuff, as did most reporters, but that meant she'd wind up in the middle of more trouble than she could handle. Of course the real reason the storm was a godsend was that he liked being with her a lot more than he should.

He grabbed the picnic basket and she swept up the blanket. "Think you can outrun the storm?" he called over the gusts.

"It's just a blow right now. In twenty minutes it'll be a downpour, and you'll be safe in your restaurant. But I'll see you later, right?"

"You bet." That gave him a few hours to get himself together and steel himself against Dixie. He needed to stick to the plan. No more near kisses. He was here on business, FBI business. And then he was gone.

DIXIE GLARED at herself in the mirror, candlelight flickering with her reflection. "Okay, this is the second time in less that twenty-four hours that I've had a hair-repair emergency. This never happened when Jan was here. With Jan, I was a hair queen."

Gracie stood behind, her gaze meeting Dixie's in the mirror, giving her the younger-sister eye roll. "Why in the world didn't you call me in when you dyed your hair in the first place?"

"You were reading to the kids. The packages had directions."

"Too bad you didn't follow them." She picked up a handful of Dixie's hair and examined it. "Well, this time it's more red—or is that rust?"

"Your reassurance overwhelms me."

"Well, I can't tell till it dries. And that's not going to happen with the electricity still out. I guess it could be worse. I trimmed Gia Maxwell's hair this afternoon. She tried to cut it herself with her vacuum cleaner. Thought if she sucked up a chunk of hair and cut, the ends would disappear into the hose, a no-mess salon treatment. She looked like a schnauzer on steroids. I evened her up. If that Nick guy wasn't such a hottie, we'd probably hang him up by his privates." Gracie grinned and tilted her head. "At least that would be some consolation. We'd all get a good view of the real man instead of speculating. He sure fills out a pair of jeans nice…going and coming."

A picture of Nick doing just that flashed through Dixie's brain, making her hot, then cold, then hot again. She thought of holding his hand, his body close to hers, the…kiss. Holy cow! The kiss. "You really like this salon stuff, don't you?"

"I think it started in kindergarten when I gave our cat a Mohawk. Remember? That was one honked-off cat."

She smiled at Gracie through the dim light. She was too thin. Worried too much. "You know you like the women and the talk and being home with the kids. You need to consider doing this hair and nail stuff full-time."

Gracie fidgeted and bit her bottom lip. "I…I can't do a salon. Running a business takes talent and good sense, and I haven't got those things. I'm just—"

"A wonderful bright person who can do whatever she sets her mind to. And you thinking otherwise is that donkey-brained ex talking. Glen ran your self-esteem into the ground. Made you believe the only thing you were good for was waiting on him hand and foot. If you hadn't found that second mortgage he took out on the house to go gambling in Vegas, he'd still be here ruining you."

"Danny running off with that model didn't do much to bolster your confidence, either."

"Touché." Dixie gripped her sister's hand and they sat on the edge of the bathtub. "We're better than this, Gracie. I'm getting my life together, and so can you. You already have a flair for hair. Hey, you can call the place the Hair Flair. Makes more sense than the Curly Cactus. Remodel the basement and open up a shop. I'll be your first customer." She laughed. "I already am. Bet you could have Jan's salon stuff cheap. Sign up for classes in Billings. I'll pay."

Gracie gazed at the floor. "I can't go back to school. I'm thirty-five. I don't think I can study anymore. My brain's oatmeal. And you sure don't have any extra money for me to go to school."

"Oh honey, you'd be surprised what I have." Or almost have. Dixie kissed her sister on the cheek. "What's taking that electricity company so long to get the lights back on? Connect a few wires, throw a switch. What's the big deal?"

"We could build a fire in the hearth for heat. You'll wind up with a head full of curls, but they'll be dry curls. Why so impatient? Got a hot date for tonight?"

"Would you believe Mr. Going-and-coming?"

Gracie's eyes danced. "You dog! You are some fast worker. How'd that happen? I need details here."

"I convinced him to go on picnic with me to the

old depot. And—this is the good part—I found a clue linking that site to the knockoff purse little Drew found. Here, I'll show you." She reached into her pocket and connected with… *Nothing?*

"Oh, no." She stood and checked all her pockets. "I don't believe it. I got a bogus registration card for a Kate Spade purse, proving I'm on the right track, and Nick Romero kept it."

She faced Gracie. "Blast that man. I'm missing something about that guy. Something big. I can feel it in my bones."

"Yeah, you're missing that he's handsome and you're going on a date and he probably just forgot to give you back your card. Why would he want a card like that anyway? It's no value to anyone." Gracie gave her a sassy wink. "Did you flirt?"

"Some. A little. I always flirt. I have a dominant flirt gene."

"Well, there you go. A card from a purse is not what's on his mind. You are."

"I don't think so. Heck, the man wouldn't even kiss me. Said he wasn't ready. What does that mean? Ready for what? It was just a kiss. Besides, men are always ready for women. Not ready sounded like one of those girly excuses. He told me he didn't know Jack, but I got a feeling that's a lie too. Nick makes strange phone calls, has people over late at night and he's a new guy in town—least, he says he doesn't, and…and…." Chuckling, she stood. "I've got it! A plan to get my card back and find out what that man's hiding."

"You'll ask him? Asking's good. Trouble-free, straigt-forward."

"Only if I need convenient answers—which I don't. He'll lie again. I'll snoop. I'll get Nick to invite me over tonight."

"Oh, girl. You're going to show him the Montana two-step, aren't you? Get him all hot and bothered and this time make him more ready for a kiss than he's ever been in his life."

"Actually, I intend to use the two-step to make him hungry. Then he can cook and I can poke around at his place and see what's up."

Gracie shook her head. "This is not a good idea, Dix. You don't know the guy, and if he is hiding something, you better be careful. What if he catches you? He could be an ax murderer."

"The man's got something I want."

Gracie fanned herself with her hand. "Oh, that man's got something we all want."

Dixie pulled Gracie up beside her. "Let's build that fire and dry my hair. It's going to be a real interesting night with Mr. Romero."

NICK AIMED his flashlight at the floor and looked at the boots he'd bought as part of his fitting-in program. They hurt. Why would anyone wear boots instead of Nikes? He'd bought new dark jeans and western-cut shirts for this gig. He looked like a gay mob boss! Italian men were not made for cowboy gear. There should be a law.

He put on the Stetson—another bad addition. He'd never done western undercover. He'd done businessman, street thug, truck driver, taxi driver, drug-gun dealer and cook on more occasions than he could count because he could really do the job. How the hell had he drawn *High Noon* in Whistlers Bend for his last assignment?

The one good thing about the electricity being out was that he couldn't see the mess he called home. The moving guys had dumped the boxes and few pieces of furniture. He'd managed to unpack a few clothes and store the samples of the knockoff designer goods in the back of the closet in his room before the electricity had died. He'd unpack the rest tomorrow.

Another rumble of thunder rattled the windowpanes in the building as he shrugged into his denim jacket. He clumped down the steps and onto the stoop. The rain slackened as he directed his flashlight at a torrent of water gushing down the street, nearly spilling onto the sidewalk. Montana in the monsoon season.

He turned up his collar and ran for the Cut Loose

at the end of the street. He doubted Dixie would show, but he needed to get to know the townfolk, be one of the group. When guys drank, they said stuff they usually wouldn't, let things slip and then didn't remember what the hell they said.

He thought of Dixie. She was the most feminine woman he'd ever met. No matter what she did, it was…girly. The way she talked, her hands always in motion, keeping time with what she said. The curious look in her eyes that made them sparkle. Her clothes that dipped in the right places and clung just where they were supposed to. His gut tightened. Damn, why couldn't she wear baggy stuff? Much easier to forget baggy.

Oil lamps, candles and a crowd filled the saloon. Lack of electricity was obviously not a big deal in Whistlers Bend. A fiddler and banjo player were tuning their instruments as Dixie sauntered up and slipped her arm through his. "Well, howdy, handsome. Buy a girl a warm beer? That's all there is tonight."

She smelled so good; even mixed with the odors of beer, tobacco, leather and cowboys, her scent intoxicated him. She looked great in her white Stetson, curls springing everywhere, framing her face and her big brown eyes. "Nice hair."

"Gracie saved me. She's my sister. I live with her and her two kids and Brutus."

"Husband?"

"Hampster with an attitude. Wanna dance?" She gave him that sexy twitch of her hips that made his head spin.

Dance? He'd been through shoot-outs where he'd narrowly escaped with his body parts intact, car chases that rivaled anything conjured up in Hollywood, clandestine meetings De Niro would envy, but none of these things unglued him like one twitch of Dixie Carmichael's hips.

The musicians struck up a tune, and she snagged his hand and shimmied her shoulders. Her eyes turned…sultry? "Holy crap," he muttered. She must have heard, because she laughed.

She started some line dance as others came onto the floor. No one moved like Dixie, her clever feet keeping perfect time and her sweet body rotating close to his, then backing away, teasing, tormenting but not touching.

He didn't want to dance. He wanted to take her in his arms, feel her next to him and kiss her senseless…*except, in no way did that fit in with undercover work!*

Everyone was watching her…and him. He had to do *something*. He had to blend. Standing there like some stupid city slicker was not working. But dance? When in Rome, do whatever the hell needs to be done to survive. But if he danced with her, they'd be body to body, and that was no way to survive anything.

People were waiting. It had been a while since he'd danced—like, over twenty years. He remembered Helen Camello. She'd outweighed him by fifty pounds and had had two left feet, but he'd always danced with her at every Italian wedding in the north end. She'd needed a break and dancing with her had made up for some of the not-so-great things he'd done as a Detroit street punk before Nonna Celest had gotten hold of him.

Who would have thought that after all these years Helen had done him a big favor, too. Nick took hold of Dixie and fell into step. Her eyes twinkled. "Hey, you're good at this, for a Denver boy."

He threw in a few fancy moves, adding a little Italian bravado that he hoped didn't throw his back out or look like a poor imitation from *The Godfather*.

He spun around, slid her in a fast two-step that landed her in his line as he claimed her space on the other side. She laughed, dancers clapped and the musicians kicked up the tempo. Damn, he loved having his hands on her.

"Where'd you learn to dance like this?" she asked with a shake of her head that sent her curls in a jig all their own.

"Denver isn't all that far away." And neither was the Italian hub of Boston. The music ended and Dixie swaggered up to him. "'Bout that beer…."

The fiddle picked up another tune. "And miss a dance?" He took her hand. "Come on."

It wasn't that he suddenly loved the Montana two-step, but it kept him moving. Sitting with Dixie had trouble all over it. How could he keep his hands off her if she and he were huddled together at the bar? He'd want to put her fingers in his, play with her curls....

He danced faster and harder to get his mind off her. At this rate he'd be dancing till he dropped dead. Trouble was, he'd still be thinking of her.

"Enough," she said, panting as the music died. "I could do with some refueling."

All he could think about was another kiss. And he needed a kiss! *No way.* Not that he'd never kissed a woman on an assignment before; he'd just never wanted to this much. Dixie clouded his brain, made him forget he was here on business and not to be with her. He pointed to the musicians as the banjo player let out with a song about a sexy woman and a horny guy. Couldn't it have been about a dog or horse or cowboy on the trail? She tugged him toward the bar.

He tugged back. Switched their hats in a playful gesture and said, "Hey, this is my favorite song," and pulled her into a series of stomps and swings. He was so tired he could barely walk, until Dixie gave him a coy look, held her hands high and did a series of fancy steps of her own that sent the place into a frenzy of wolf whistles.

She was the hottest, sexiest female in the bar, probably all of Montana, maybe the United States.

Why not a wallflower? Why so tempting? The only solution was to wind this case up real damn fast!

The dance ended. She sagged into his arms and gazed up at him, grinning. "I need food."

I need a tranquilizer. "I'll see if Ray will get you a sandwich."

"I was thinking about that dinner you promised. You could cook for me now."

"As in tonight?" Being alone in his house with Dixie was not a good idea. "No electricity, sweetheart."

As if on cue, the lights blinked, then came on. The FBI gods hated him—revenge for taking early retirement. Everyone clapped and cheered for the electric company, and Dixie put her arm around Nick's waist and led him toward the door. "It's your duty to feed me, show me that giving up the Curly Cactus for Nick's was worth it. I didn't have dinner." She gazed up at him. "Surely you can provide for a starving woman."

He was doomed. No way could he get out of this one. He had to whip up something for her at his place with no one else around.

Okay, he reasoned. He'd do it, then send her on her way. "How's Spaghetti Mediterranean sound?"

"Complicated." She shuffled out the door, pulling him with her. He had to keep her talking to get focused on her words and not on her. They got to the sidewalk and he said, "Tell me about the town, the part I haven't seen."

The humidity gave the streetlights a fuzzy halo. Moisture covered everything, giving it a fresh clean appearance.

"Well," Dixie said as she took his hand in hers, making him a little wobbly. "Not much to tell. You saw the depot and mountains. We have ranchers like Maggie, and a doctor." Dixie pointed to the next street. "BJ's house and office are down there. Across the street is the bank. *Whistle Stop* is the town news-paper and now we have Nick's."

"And lots of wide-open spaces."

"Of course. That's the charm of Montana."

And that was what made it nearly impossible to find trucks meeting up in the middle of the night. Dixie paused under the streetlight, droplets clinging to her lashes, her brown eyes bigger than ever. He let go of her hand to regain his equilibrium—at least give it a try. "Why are you a reporter?"

"Why are you a cook? You like discovering new dishes. I like discovering a good story."

He touched a curl at her cheek because he forgot he shouldn't and he really wanted the connection. "What really makes Dixie Carmichael tick?"

"I can't resist poking my nose in where it doesn't belong—ask anybody in town. But I didn't realize I wanted to do it for a living till lately."

"Read one of those getting-in-tune-with-your-inner-self books?"

"A potential glitch jolted me out of a three-year coma that was a side effect from a messy divorce. I decided to get on with the business of living, doing what I really wanted because wallowing in self-pity wasn't getting me anywhere."

"Can't imagine you doing the pity routine. You're too…" *Feisty, energetic, fun.* And he wanted to kiss her so bad he could almost taste her lips on his. "We should eat."

He stepped onto the stoop and unlocked the door to the future Nick's Place.

"I'm too what?" she asked, not moving from under the light. "You never finished the sentence."

You're too everything, he thought, but said, "You're probably hungry. I am. All that dancing did me in." He couldn't tell her what was really on his mind. It was too intimate and he couldn't go there. He'd get lost in Dixie and never find his way out. He flipped the switch on the wall, the bare bulbs casting harsh shadows. "Come on. I'll show you my pots."

"First time I've ever heard that line." She laughed and stepped into the room, and he nodded to the back. "Kitchen's that way."

But instead of heading there, she took off her hat, letting her incredible curls tumble free as she gazed around. "So, how are you going to decorate the place now that you got rid of all Jan's stuff? It doesn't smell so much like perm solution now. When you tear up the carpet, it will be even better."

"Decorate?" Needles of panic pricked his spine. He'd planned on acquiring restaurant stuff, not putting it all together. Didn't think he'd be around long enough for that. If she wasn't driving him crazy with her delicious body, she was asking questions he didn't have answers to.

She pressed. "You know, as in fix up this place like a restaurant? Ambience. Décor. What are your plans, Nick Romero? Surely you have plans."

She put her hat on the ladder he'd left standing in the middle of the room and ran her hands through her hair. He grinned while struggling for an answer. He wasn't a decorator. He didn't even have pictures on his walls in his apartment—and he'd lived there five years. To him decorating was putting the toilet paper roll on the spindle, instead of setting it on the sink.

What would Nonna Celest do with this place? He'd spent years surrounded by paint chips, swatches of material, furniture catalogs and magazines, rolled carpets leaning against the wall. Something had to have rubbed off on him, soaked into his brain.

"I'm doing a bistro effect." *Okay, that was good. Keep going.* "Maybe saffron-yellow stucco walls, parchment-white beam ceilings that are lower, giving it an intimate garden feel." No doubt, this was the first time an FBI agent had uttered the phrase *inti-*

mate garden feel. "And some plants that can wind around the beams and white columns. Tear up this old carpet and put in Florida tiles. Gardenias." Celest kept gardenias, made the place smell like heaven. He'd almost forgotten till now. "Wine-colored Roman shades at the windows, sage green trim. Candles."

She smiled. "In wine bottles?"

He smiled back, because whenever she smiled, he wanted to, too. "Why not. Candles in bottles and tablecloths to match the shades. I never was into that checkered thing." He found one of the catalogs he'd brought to make it look as if he truly was opening a restaurant. He opened to a place he'd marked. "Here are the dishes and the wineglasses and the linens."

She pointed to the tableware with a white pattern with a basket weave pattern. "This is great. When does the kitchen equipment get here? I'm sure you'll have to update the appliances."

Something flickered in her eyes, as if this was a trick question. Wasn't she buying his great story? Hell, it sounded good to him. He'd just decorated the whole flipping restaurant for her. What more did she want? "Soon, very soon. For now we can use the stove and fridge that are here."

He cupped her elbow and led her toward the kitchen. Enough with the questions. He needed some action, diversion. "Let's cook. How's that sound to a hungry woman?"

PERFECT, Dixie decided as she went with Nick into the kitchen. He tucked a towel into the waistband of his jeans as if he'd done it a million times, then pulled an armful of veggies from the fridge. He nodded at a pile of boxes on the floor beside a table and four chairs. "You want to grab a pot? They're in there."

"I don't believe it. You really did want to show me your pots."

"If I hadn't, that would have been the worst pickup line in history."

She laughed as she undid the box flaps and unwound bubble-wrap, exposing a big shiny silver pan. "Pasta pot. Expensive brushed aluminum."

He glanced back. "Mind filling it up with water and putting it on the stove? The two-quart saucier should be in there, too."

"Saucier? Sounds like a British lady of the night." She ran the tap. "I use cookware I buy from the grocery store on the sale racks."

"This is All-Clad. Ideal pots for the ideal kitchen. Cooking is relaxing, immediately gratifying, and you can eat your creation. Works for me."

"My ideal kitchen has a fridge, microwave and garbage can. I nuke, I eat, I pitch."

"You didn't cook for your family?" He washed the saucier.

"I cooked a lot. I just don't like to."

He withdrew a knife from a cutlery block, put the tomatoes on a wooden board and slit them into halves with the precision of a surgeon, then cleaned out the seeds. No squashed tomato parts oozing all over.

"Okay, I'm impressed. You really are a good cook."

He flashed a male grin that made her hair curl even more. "It helps when you're trying to open a restaurant."

No canned soup and grilled cheese here. *But...* There was still that *but* nagging at her. Was it the look in his eyes? The overhead light in the kitchen played in his dark, rich hair, and his back was sure and strong as he bent over the stove.

He was so handsome. Maybe she should forget the niggling feeling. Maybe she should just enjoy the handsome, intelligent, good cook, laid-back, easygoing man the way Maggie had suggested. Maybe there was nothing up with the guy at all; maybe his terrific attributes short-circuited her ability to sniff out trouble and she was imagining there being something up with Nick.

There was only one way to find out for sure if any of those *maybes* were true. "Mind if I use the little girl's room?"

He gathered the diced tomatoes into his hands and dropped them into the saucier. "In this case it's the little boy's room, too." He grabbed parsley. "Next door past the stairs. But you probably knew that. Help yourself."

Nice that he offered, because that was exactly what she intended to do.

Chapter Four

Bypassing the bathroom, she took the stairs, stepping on the edges to minimize squeaking—something she'd learned when sneaking into her own house as a teenager and she was out after curfew. Only one small squeak escaped, not enough to give her away. Although she wouldn't have been surprised if Nick had heard her heart beating louder than the thunder that had echoed through the town earlier.

She reached the top landing and gulped air to steady her nerves. *Get a grip, girl!* This was all part of investigative reporting. And so was getting shot for trespassing, except Nick didn't seem like the shooting type. Then again, what type was he?

She flipped on the light. Boxes everywhere. Typical moving scenario. A fast rummage through them would take way more time than she had right now. Breaking and entering loomed in her future.

"Dixie?" Nick's voice sounded from below.

She turned off the light in the room and scurried on tiptoes to the top of the stairs as Nick appeared at the bottom. *Excuse!* She needed an excuse for what the heck she was doing up here. He turned on the hall light, flooding the faded wallpaper and dark wood in harsh rays. He gazed up at her, a questioning look on his face. She babbled, "I…uh…" *Think, Dixie, think!*

"Needed towels?" he offered. "I wasn't expecting company and didn't put any fresh ones out. I just remembered."

She beamed. "Well, you can't think of everything. Now, can you? You've just moved in." *Saved by the towel.* "I didn't want to bother since you were cooking, so I decided to use the bathroom up here."

She descended the stairs, the planks creaking as she went. Nick didn't back away from the bottom but blocked her path. Was he onto her? His dark black eyes told her he was suspicious. She didn't need suspicious. She needed gullible. Her insides squirmed and she resisted the urge to run. Investigative reporters did not run; they sucked it up and looked brave. Lois Lane always looked very brave. And with such an ugly hairdo she'd probably had lots of practice. "Is…is that tomatoes I smell boiling?"

"Damn—the sauce." He tore back to the kitchen and she sagged against the wall. She had to get better at this lying stuff. If Nick realized she was digging around in his things, he'd never let down his guard and she'd never figure him out.

She headed for the kitchen. The best part of all this was she now had two adventures going on at once: the smugglers *and* Nick. She watched him stirring the sauce, and her heart beat faster and harder. Even without an adventure, she'd like having this man in her life. "Did your sauce burn?"

"Close. Do you like anchovies and green olives and capers in your sauce?"

"Never had them together, but I figure I'm about to." She drew up beside him so as to peek in the pot. Who was she kidding? This was an excuse to get close to him.

He added fresh basil and oregano. "Mind stirring the spaghetti so it doesn't clump?"

She found a wooden spoon. "Everything smells great." *Including you.*

He turned the dark red concoction to simmer, picked glasses and utensils from the cabinet and drawers, and set everything on the little table. He took the spoon from her fingers, caught a strand of spaghetti on the side and slurped it into this mouth, the thin white strand disappearing till he bit off the end and put it to her lips. "Your turn. What's your opinion?"

That she was ready to lose her mind with his fingers so close to her lips. Her tongue caught the noodle, grazing his thumb, and her insides did a slow burn like the sauce bubbling on the stove. His gaze held hers. She tried to swallow, but the spaghetti caught in her dry throat, making her choke, breaking the spell.

Thank heavens! Not that she wanted to choke to death, but something had to come between them before… Before what? Before she jumped into his arms and kissed him senseless and they did the horizontal hula right there on his kitchen floor.

He got a glass and filled it with water. "Are you okay?" he asked as he handed it to her.

She gulped the water down. "I'm fine. Terrific. Let's eat."

He snagged the stockpot with two towels and dumped the spaghetti into the colander to drain it, then set the colander back into the pot. He winked. "Keeps it warm. There's a selection of wines in the closet."

And that was where they should stay. She did not need wine and Nick and good food all at the same time. "If it's not wine in a box I'm clueless—one of the reasons my ex ditched me."

"Because you didn't know wine?"

"Because I wasn't the sophisticated type he wanted. After he got stinking rich, that mattered." She claimed a chair and Nick served a plate of the most heavenly smelling pasta on earth. He filled his own plate, then popped a cork from the bottle he'd retrieved.

"A '97 Panzanetto Castelluccio. One of my favorite Italian wines. My grandmother lives close to this vineyard. She took a vacation to Florence, fell in love and never came back." He smiled. "You'd like her." He poured the wine and Dixie ate an olive to keep from salivating over him. Tall, dark, handsome, a wine connoisseur and he could cook and loved his grandmother.

He was incredible and more. The *more* was what worried her. "You know," she said as she dug into the food and twirled the spaghetti, making sure not to lose any anchovies or olives, "today when we were up at the depot, you kept that Kate Spade card I found."

He twirled pasta, not missing a beat. "Hey, you're right. I did. And I have the hat that you lent me, too. I'll get them after we eat. They're upstairs in my closet."

He devoured a forkful. "We should talk about the 5-K run. You need to decide on a route, get volunteers to stand along the way and pass out water. Get some promo out there so people will register."

See, she said to herself, *the card was an innocent oversight.* And Nick was concerned about the run, getting involved and helping with it. One of the good guys…or just a good front.

Darn it! Why couldn't she get beyond that feeling?

She smiled sweetly, genuinely. She'd give his place a thorough going-through when he wasn't around and prove to herself beyond a doubt what had her antsy about Nick Romero was simply her overactive imagination or basic female lust. Then she could get to know him better…a lot better. At least for a while.

But then she had things to do, places to go. At forty she wasn't after a permanent relationship—been there, done that—and Nick Romero didn't have that yearning-to-be-settled look about him, either. All she had to do was get rid of this unsettled feeling she had about the man, then sit back and enjoy the fun.

NICK TOOK A LONG DRINK of the Panzanetto and studied Dixie as she ate and talked about Whistlers Bend. She reminded him of a glass of fine wine—robust, full-flavored, a little mysterious—and potentially addictive as hell. How could he stay focused on his work with Dixie around? He couldn't! He had to keep their time together at a minimum, that was the answer. Only be together when necessary.

"Gee, it's getting late," he said to Dixie. "Your sister will wonder where you are."

"Not really." He tried not to notice Dixie's full lush lips on the wineglass, and shoved three bites of spaghetti into his mouth.

She arched an eyebrow. "Hungry?"

"Tired," he said around a mouthful. "Very tired." *And suddenly horny.*

Dixie was way too distracting. But he couldn't walk away altogether. She was familiar with the area and was damn good at stumbling across clues. More important, she shouldn't be out looking for clues alone. Way too dangerous.

He needed to watch out for her and that meant staying focused and thinking of Dixie as *the job,* except that was hard with her licking sauce from her lips. Did she have to do that? He needed to get this assignment finished!

He'd get ahold of Wes and show him the registration card. Since Wes was staying in Rocky Fork, keeping an eye on things there and fronting as a freelance photographer, he could drive over later tonight. Nick scarfed down another spun forkful of spaghetti not taking time to really taste and savor. What a waste of good food and beautiful company.

She was staring at him wide-eyed now. "Fast eater."

He shoveled in two more portions of food, stifled a burp sat back and patted his gut. "You almost finished?"

She glanced at her half-eaten portion. "Well, I—"

"Good." He stood. "I'll pack you a doggie bag."

She steepled her fingers. "Okay, Romero. What's wrong? It's like you suddenly want to get rid of me."

She held up her hands in surrender. "Just say the word and I'm out of here. You don't have to suffer acute indigestion on my part. I can take a hint."

"I'm—" *Really nuts about you and can't keep my mind on my work* is what he thought. But instead he said, "I'm just…getting over a relationship. Having trouble adjusting…to…women. But I do want to see you. The time at the depot was great. I like being part of your investigations. I'm kind of a private person, not real adventuresome."

Hell, at least the "private person" was true.

She stood, looking more sympathetic. He felt like a rat! "I understand breaking up. I really do. When Danny left me it was awful."

Awful! Nick clenched his jaw. Dixie didn't deserve awful. She walked over to him, touched his shoulder, tiptoed and kissed him on the cheek. *Oh, hell.* Her lips were warm, soft and a bit moist against his skin. Her touch gentle and tender and caring. Great! Big-city liar meets nice western girl.

He was a louse!

"I'll see you later," she said as she made for the door.

"Call me if you go off on one of your adventures, okay?"

She turned and smiled, making his insides quake. How could one smile do that to him? Then again, the smile was Dixie Carmichael's and everything about her affected him somehow. "You bet," she said. She nodded at the dishes. "I'd stay and help you clean up, but I don't think that's what you want."

"Thanks for a great evening."

She walked into the main room and he heard the soft click of the door closing behind her. He looked to the table and the lipstick smudge on her wineglass. It was a really poor substitute for her lipstick on his mouth. His arms actually ached to be around her. He licked his lips, tasting wine, knowing he'd much rather taste Dixie.

He heard footsteps in the back hallway. "Dixie?" Did he say that? Probably because he wanted it to be her. Instead, Wes stood in the entrance to the kitchen. He flashed Nick a big dopey grin, did a really bad rendition of hip twitching and said in a squeaky voice, "Hi, there, big boy. Come up and see me sometime."

Nick started to laugh, till he caught sight of Dixie behind Wes. She stood there spellbound. She finally managed to say, "Uh, I forgot my hat and heard voices and…" She held up the hat. "Didn't mean to interrupt."

Cripes. The plan was for him and Wes never to be seen together. Two strangers in town at the same time were too hard to explain. Well, he'd better do some fast explaining now! "Dixie," he said in a rush, "this is Wes. He's a freelance photographer over in Rocky Fork. He's going to take pictures of Nick's Place when it's done and some of the entrees and desserts on the menu. Help me get ads together. He stopped by to set up a time."

Dixie smiled, but it was one of those you-think-I'm-buying-this-load-of-bull smiles. He needed to convince her. "Wes and I knew each other in Denver."

Wes fished a business card from his pocket. "If you have a job for a photographer, I'm your man. I'll be in the area for a month or so. Doing a piece on small northwest towns. I happened to be in Whistlers Bend tonight and thought I'd pay a visit to old Nick."

Wes held out a hand to Dixie. "Glad to meet you—"

"Dixie Carmichael," she supplied, and took his hand. She seemed a little more convinced he was telling the truth. Wes's smile could convince any woman of anything. And why did he suddenly want to punch Wes in the nose for smiling at Dixie? *He needed a shrink!*

"I'll be on my way," Dixie said as she pocketed the card. "And I'll keep you in mind for pictures. Thanks."

She left, and Nick waited for the final click of the door. He ducked around Wes to make sure the door latched for real this time. Tomorrow it got fixed!

Wes said, "Damn! I saw Dixie leave, I thought the coast was clear to come in. When I looked in the window you two sure seemed to be getting along."

Nick raked back his hair. "That is the most inquisitive woman on planet Earth. Hope we convinced her we are who we say we are. She's a reporter and never keeps things quiet. The good news is she's also probably related to Sherlock Holmes. If there's a clue somewhere around, she finds it."

Wes dumped the remaining spaghetti onto a plate and added the rest of the sauce. He sat at the table and dug in. "This is great," Wes mumbled around a mouthful. "I'm starved."

"No kidding."

Wes glanced up, grinning like a big bear. "Damn, you're a good cook. Can't wait till you really open a restaurant."

"Can't wait till you really start that book on the West you're always talking about."

Wes shook his head and shoveled in more pasta. "Don't have time for that. I can't imagine leaving the bureau."

"Even with a slug in your shoulder?"

"Occupational hazard. I'm fine. Never better."

Right, Nick thought, Wes should get out of the FBI now, find a life. He was a good guy, a friend going on twenty years and Nick's partner for the past ten. How long would his luck hold before all his near misses caught up with him? But Wes wasn't listening. Nick was all too aware of that.

Nick reached into his back pocket and pulled out

the fake card. "Dixie found this up at the abandoned depot outside of town. It's in decent shape, which means it's new. I think our smugglers used that spot to off-load merchandise from big trucks to smaller ones. Have you found anything over in Rocky Fork?"

Wes eyed the card and swiped a napkin across his mouth. "Hell, nothing as good as this. I'm betting that even if the smugglers are using other locations in the area, sooner or later they'll rotate back to ones they've used before. The big question is—when will they rotate?"

He leaned back in the chair, and Nick handed him a glass of wine as he continued. "I got a call this morning. U.S. Customs and Immigration agents busted seventeen people for smuggling fifty million dollars' worth of bogus Louis Vuitton, Prada, Coach, Chanel, Christian Dior and Fendi merchandise in thirty forty-foot containers through Port Elizabeth, New Jersey. The smugglers are part of a crime network and the money was traced to accounts that fund known terrorist groups in the Middle East."

"Why in the hell would someone buy this fake junk when the money goes to organizations sworn to destroy them?"

"They say the knockoff rage is sport. Do you believe that? Sport! A very deadly sport."

"I'll stop by tomorrow and show Jack the card to keep him in the loop. I'll do it on the sly. If Dixie sees

me with Jack too much, she'll start putting things together and figure out who I am."

Wes sat back and let out a contented sigh. "I can
tell by the way she focused on you that there's more
than spaghetti cooking between you two."

"Nothing but business."

Wes chuckled softly as he stood and turned for the
hallway. "Watch yourself, partner. You don't want
any distractions on the job." He massaged his shoulder. "One of us nearly buying it is enough."

Nick listened to the back door close. Wes was
right. Dixie Carmichael had turned his brain to mush
and he'd better get over it fast. Too much depended
on his finding the smugglers that would help put an
end to a really nasty business and keep Dixie safe.

DIXIE POURED Maggie a cup of coffee as the morning
crowd drifted into the Purple Sage. "I need a favor."

Maggie groaned. "I could tell there was some reason you wanted me to stop here before my cattle
ranchers' meeting. I was hoping you discovered the
perfect wedding dress." She winked at Dixie. "Heard
you gave Gracie the five-hundred bucks you won to
take cosmetology classes."

"They start on Saturday." Dixie fluffed her curls.
"Now we're all saved. And if you help me out, I'll
get her to do your hair for your wedding free and I'll
really concentrate on that perfect dress. I swear."

"A bribe?" Maggie wiggled her brows. "This must be one doozy of a favor."

"It's just a tiny little one." Dixie sat across the table and leaned toward Maggie, keeping her voice low. "My shift here is done in twenty minutes. All I need is one hour alone in Nick's place. You have the cattle ranchers' meeting at ten. Just call Nick and tell him you want to introduce him to the ranchers. That it'll be good for his restaurant business and he can buy beef direct. Or whatever you want to tell him. Make up something so I can rummage through his house. I felt something was not right with that guy before, but now… Well, it's worse than ever and I want to figure out what he's up to."

"This is because of that other guy showing up last night, isn't it? I knew when you mentioned him on the phone that there was a new bee in your bonnet. Nick's a cook, Dix. The other guy is a photographer. They were friends in Denver. Doesn't sound all that strange an explanation to me. We get photographers here all the time, thanks to that *Horse Whisperer* movie that showed how gorgeous it is in Montana. In my opinion, that feeling you have about Nick is…*amore*. Steamy Italian vibes. Enjoy the ride, girl."

"Just give me an hour, and when I don't find anything, I'll forget about investigating Nick and maybe go for that ride—at least till I have to leave." She let out a sigh. "But to tell you the truth, Nick's not as steamy as you think. He's getting over a relationship, and all but tossed me out of his house last night because he wasn't ready. First he passes on my kiss and now this. Holy cow! Maybe I'm losing my touch."

"Are you kidding? You're just what he needs to get over a relationship. A little fun, a little sass. But forget the snooping, okay?"

"I can't. It's an obsession. Some people have chocolate obsessions. I have—"

"A buttinski obsession a mile wide."

She handed over Nick's number. "Got this from one of the clerks over at the bank. He got it from the mortgage statement. Make the call. Someone said they saw him downstairs, tearing up the old carpet. The meeting's in a half hour. When this is over and done with and I won't pester you anymore."

"That's because I'll be dead. Jack's the sheriff. I'm his wife…well, almost wife. I shouldn't be doing this. Isn't aiding a break-in against the law?"

"You're not breaking in. I am. All you're doing is inviting a man to a meeting. Jack won't find out. And if he does, making up will be so much fun. I just got to get rid of this nagging feeling I have about Nick. The man's driving me nuts. And it's more than his Italian studliness!"

Maggie puffed out a big breath. "All right, all right. Because we're friends." She punched in the numbers. "You better find me the best dress ever. You owe me."

Dixie listened to the one-sided conversation as Maggie charmed Nick and got him to agree to come to the meeting. She disconnected. "It's done, but if Jack strangles me I'm coming back to haunt you, and it won't be pretty."

Maggie left for her meeting, and Dixie poured more coffee for customers and served up two orders of Sunrise Skillet and two of Mile-high Hotcakes before her shift ended. She changed into jeans and headed for Nick's. She plastered a big smile on her face and knocked on the back door like any good neighbor paying a visit. When Nick didn't answer, she found the key Jan had hidden under the rock in the garden and unlocked the back door. At least, she tried to. The key didn't work.

How interesting was that! So, Nick Romero didn't like her coming back last night and finding him with that Wes guy. Why? Who was this guy? She stepped back and eyed an open upstairs window and the pine tree next to the building, with branches from ground to roof. She stepped onto the bottom branch, close to the trunk so the thin branch would support her, and climbed. More shades of teenage years and missing curfew. Except then she'd been young and in good shape.

She got to the roof and crawled on all fours across

the shingles to the window. A screen? She needed to start packing breaking-and-entering equipment when she did things like this. She wedged her fingernails between the screen frame and window frame and shoved sideways. Three fingernails snapped and the screen popped out. She laid the screen on the roof and slipped inside to the back bedroom. Empty. Nothing to look at here. Nick's bedroom was in the front.

She checked her watch. Forty minutes left, and Maggie better keep Nick busy that long. Boxes still littered the floor of his room. No dresser, bed unmade. She dug through the boxes—shirts, jeans, all neat and new. He was a briefs, not a boxer, man. Blue and gray and black ones. Not a tighty-whitey in sight. Her fingers lingered on the soft cotton. Then she thought of what that soft cotton held. A great butt…and more. *Oh, so much more!*

She swallowed, heat rushing to all body parts. It had been a while since she'd been in the company of more. *Not now, Carmichael. Think about that later.* She had twenty minutes left, with zilch to show for her efforts so far…except palpitations over Nick.

She opened the closet. Jackets, a few pair of jeans that had made it to a hanger, the baseball cap she'd lent him. She picked it off the shelf. Maybe he put that registration card in the cap to return to her later. She turned it over as she heard the front door open, then close.

Nick! Cripes! She fumbled the hat and it fell to the floor. She bent to get it, and caught a glimpse of a box shoved into the back of the closet, out of the way. Why there?

Nick's footsteps sounded on the stairs. Good thing he didn't use her step-on-the-edge trick or she never would have heard him. She pulled on the door but didn't close it all the way in case it squeaked or clicked shut. She prayed he didn't look in the back bedroom and notice that the screen was out. Her pulse beat fast in her temple. A migraine threatened right along with a stroke. She had nerves of jelly. The gals on *Alias* never had nerves of jelly. *Buck up, Carmichael!*

She peeked through the crack as Nick walked in and sat on the bed. He pulled out his cell phone and punched up a number, leaned his forearms on his knees and said, "Hey, I'm going to need restaurant equipment and furniture. Can you get it delivered? Dixie coming in on us together wasn't in the plan, but now that she has, it's okay if you come around. We can act like friends without causing suspicion." He listened, then replied, "Yeah, I'm making changes as I go. This isn't as easy as I thought it would be. I have to prove to everyone I'm just one of the good old boys."

He disconnected, ran his hand back and forth over his head in a frustrated manner. He puffed out a breath, muttered something about this being a pain, stood and left, his footfalls retreating down the steps. The front door closed, and she hurried to the window in time to see Nick cut across the street to the hardware store. What was all that about his needing changing? Change what? And how did this affect that Wes guy? That was obviously who he was talking to.

But right now she had to get out of here before Nick returned. She didn't want to try her luck a second time at hiding. She eyed the closet, and again glimpsed the big box in the back. Just a quick peek inside would satisfy her curiosity. She scooted the box out and pulled apart the flaps. More bubble wrap. The man was king of bubble wrap. She dug further and yanked out— "A purse?" Not just a purse but Prada.

She rummaged around more and slid another purse out. "Louis Vuitton." She held it by the handle and sighed. "This is so gorgeous," she whispered worshipfully.

She put it on the floor beside the Prada, pawed through more bubble wrap and found a cute Coach purse in blue, then a pink Kate Spade. "Good heavens. It's Christmas! Oh, I love Kate Spade." She held it to her side and posed. She looked good with Kate. Everyone looked good with Kate!

She pushed aside more bubbles to a picture

of…Cher…then a CD of show tunes in a white gift box. Incredible scarves. Silk. Designer, complete with logo and signatures. Then a stash of perfumes! The good French stuff in pretty little glass bottles.

What in the world was Nick Romero doing with these things hidden in his closet? She wished all these beautiful things were in her closet!

Holy crap! Her heart sank. She picked up the picture of Cher and the CD featuring *Oklahoma!*, feeling worse than she had when Danny had run off with that model. Nick Romero…he wasn't who he appeared to be at all. Not that it was a bad thing. Just not what she suspected.

Nick Romero was gay!

Chapter Five

Numb after her encounter with the purses, Cher and the show tunes, Dixie boxed everything up and shoved the box back into the closet. She got the screen off the roof and slid it back into the window, then went downstairs, her brain scrambled. Confusion sat in her gut like a two-day-old jelly doughnut. She opened the door, reset the latch and closed it, then walked down the path and right into… "Nick? I was here…looking for you, and you weren't home. Gee, imagine that."

He grinned. "Well, I'm here now."

And he was. Great-fitting jeans, slim hips, broad shoulders, twinkling dark eyes. He seemed so much a…man. She said, "Dinner. I wanted to thank you for dinner. It was terrific. And Wes seems like a nice guy."

"We've known each other for years."

She mentally wept. So much manliness and not

one bit of it interested in her or anyone remotely like her. "Just thought I'd stop by. I'm meeting up with Maggie at the Sage."

"Are you okay? You're acting a little preoccupied, like something's on your mind."

"Nothing important. See you around." She turned and made her way down the stone path, sensing Nick's eyes on her as she went. She couldn't stay and talk. Talk about what? She needed to get to the Sage—familiar territory—and sort things out.

She entered the diner and slid into the seat across from Maggie. "Well," Maggie stage-whispered, her eyes sparking with excitement. "What happened? I did my bit and got him out of his place—at least, as long as I could."

BJ took a third seat. "What are we talking about? What did I miss?"

Dixie pinched the bridge of her nose and closed her eyes for a moment to collect her wits. She said in an equally low voice, "You are not going to believe this. Nick's gay."

BJ and Maggie exchanged glances, then sat back and laughed. "Sure he is," BJ said.

Dixie's spine stiffened. "You think I'd make something like that up? Good grief. The man's as gay as New Year's Eve in New York City. He cooks, has neat new clothes and keeps his hair trimmed. And he can decorate. Uses terms like *saffron yellow* and *parchment white* and *Roman shades*. I ask you, just how many straight men even know what a Roman shade is? He hates danger of any sort. He's so laid back, not an ounce of testosterone pumping through his veins, and he can dance like a dream and—"

"That is so lame. You're being shallow," Maggie interrupted. "Those are stereotypes. You can't tell if someone's gay just by appearance."

Dixie leaned closer still. "Nick's got that boyfriend, Wes. He asked Nick to come up and see him sometime, in this real flirty voice."

BJ's eyes rounded and Dixie added, "And here's the clincher. Nick has women's stuff. Really, really nice women's stuff. Prada, Chanel, Gucci. The man has excellent taste. What man has taste in anything but beer and all things grilled? Nick has designer purses, perfume, scarves to die for. Not only is the first guy I've really liked since my divorce gay, but he accessorizes better than I do!"

BJ tapped her fingers on the tabletop. "I have to admit you've got some list there. Not that being gay is a bad thing. I'm just surprised."

"*You're* surprised?" Dixie said. "How would you like to be the woman in a potential relationship and find this out? There were signs. I just didn't pick up on them. When I tried to kiss Nick he started to cooperate, then stepped away. I even held his hand for a little while, but then he let go."

Dixie sat back again. A slow smile fell across her lips. "Which means maybe he's…changing?"

Maggie leveled her a stare. "Define *changing*. Like in his address from Denver to Whistlers Bend?"

"In that he's attracted to *me*. I heard him on the phone and he admitted he was changing. Said he just couldn't do it all at once. What if he's just confused?" A grin split Dixie's face.

BJ took her hand. "Being homosexual doesn't work like that, dear. It's a preference, not a confusion."

"So, I'll get him to prefer me. I'll convert him."

BJ said, "You'll humiliate yourself and him. This is Nick's business. Let him alone, Dixie. There are other men for you out there."

"But I like this one," she whined. She didn't intend to whine. It just kind of slipped out. "What if we kidnap Nick? Technically, that would be man-napping."

"Technically, that would be twenty to life in the big house. And there is no *we* on this plan. You can't kidnap Nick. What are you thinking? For openers, he's bigger than you."

"Yeah, but he's kind of a namby-pamby. I bet we could do it if we really tried. Danny has that chalet up in the foothills he and Charity never use because Danny's too busy with work. We'll take away all Nick's clothes so he can't escape. Maggie can get a pair of Jack's handcuffs and—"

"There is no way BJ and I are going to be a party

to this hare-brained idea," Maggie groused. "Though the handcuffs would be interesting, I've got to admit."

Dixie folded her arms and pursed her lips in full pouting mode. "All right, all right, you made your point. I'll take his pots and pans hostage. Not nearly as much fun, but they'll serve the purpose. Heaven knows he'd go to the ends of the earth for his saucier!"

Maggie gave her the you-got-to-be-kidding eye roll. "Honey, no one, not even a homosexual man who loves to cook, goes after pots and pans."

Dixie tipped her chin, feeling better by the minute over her latest plan. "Wanna bet?"

DUSK HOVERED over the town as Nick tossed the last piece of old rug into his leased truck to haul into the dump. He'd worked like mad these past few days to get stuff done. He swiped sweat from his forehead. Being an agent took him to a lot of places but none as incredible as Montana. Wild, free, natural. God's country before man messed with it. Whistlers Bend restored his…soul. After all he'd seen, sometimes he doubted he even had one.

He went back inside and gazed around the empty main room. Not bad, not bad at all. Tomorrow the tile guys were scheduled to put down terra-cotta pavers and the painters would strip the ugly wallpaper in the hall and stairway, then apply the stucco façade and paint the woodwork. He'd tear out the old kitchen himself and install the new cabinets he'd ordered if he was still around. Otherwise he'd have them delivered to his real restaurant. The Viking stove and Sub-Zero refrigerator and freezer would come in a day or two. He'd picked them out online, paid for them and would take them with him after the assignment was over. Thank heaven for the Internet.

He didn't have much of a choice about doing these things. His cover of opening a restaurant and being a chef was wearing thin with nothing restaurantlike happening around here. People in small towns were nosy as hell. Knew everyone's business, especially that of the new guy who had gotten rid of their hair diva and didn't seem to be doing much else with the place.

But right now he was as hungry as a winter wolf. Where'd that expression come from? Not something he'd heard in L.A. or New York, that was for damn sure. Probably from someone at the hardware store when he'd picked out paint and gotten the names of the tile guys and painters. Or maybe it had come from one of the ranchers at the meeting that Maggie had dragged him to this morning. Then again, it could have been from the checkout man at the market— what was his name…Barney? He helped Nick select fresh produce every morning, even held some of the best tomatoes back just for him.

He was getting to know everyone, and that's what he was supposed to do. But now he was talking like them. He'd picked up gang slang fast enough; now it was Montana-ese. He liked that a lot more.

He made his way to the kitchen, and pictured Dixie sitting at the table, eating spaghetti. He'd needed every ounce of self-control to keep his hands and lips to himself that night. The past two days he'd managed to avoid her since he'd been working, and that should be a good thing—out of sight, out of mind. Except it didn't work. He missed her a lot more than he should.

He went to the box to get a saucepan to warm up leftover spaghetti from the other night, pulled back the flaps and… "Holy hell!"

"What's going on?" Sheriff Jack Dawson asked from the doorway.

Nick shook his head. "You are not going to believe this one."

Grinning, Jack took a chair at the table. "Oh, I think I am. Let's see, someone's filched your pots and left you a map telling you where to find them."

Nick put the map on the table. "And how in blue blazes the hell did you know that?"

Jack tipped the chair on two rear legs, balancing against the wall. "Somehow Dixie Carmichael has gotten it into her head that you're gay and…here's where it gets even better."

"Gay? Gay! Oh, I can't wait to hear the rest."

"She's deemed it her duty to convert you. Turn

you into a *man* for the benefit of women everywhere. Seems you're really a hunk and she doesn't want to see it wasted."

Nick went to the fridge and snagged two beers. He sat at the table and handed one to Jack. They popped the cans and drank. Nick swiped the back of his hand across his lips. "I needed that. I got to tell you that in all my years with the bureau nothing—and I do mean not one damn thing—like this has ever happened. I'm gay?"

"The situation is more like Dixie's *borrowing* your pans so you'll come to her to get them back. I have no idea what you're walking into, but I promise it won't be boring."

"Nothing about that woman is boring. She's got to be the most *un*boring person in the universe." Nick sat and leaned his elbows on the table and chuckled. "How'd you find out about the pans and what in the hell gave Dixie the idea I'm gay?"

"Dixie decided you were gay after she found your stash of knockoff purses."

Nick bolted straight up. "She broke into my house and went through my things?"

"She had a feeling you were more than just a cook and when she came across a picture of Cher and a CD with show tunes she put it all together and got…."

"Gay. The picture and music were a little bureau humor," Nick growled. "Damn."

Jack laughed. "Well, whatever happens, tonight will more than make up for any inconvenience, I can guarantee that. In fact, I just bet you're in for one incredible *conversion*. At one point handcuffs were discussed. Maggie told me all about it because she thought you should know what you're walking into."

Dixie, him, handcuffs! This was not how to get over Dixie Carmicheal. "And here I thought this was a sleepy little town in the middle of nowhere."

Jack tapped the map. "Dixie's at her ex's chalet in Cabin Springs. It's not far from the old depot, but the best way there is to go west and take a turnoff before you reach the interstates. The roads are better that way. You'll see the sign Danny's Delight. Don't know why people name their houses up here, but they do."

"Why is she doing this conversion thing? I don't get it."

"Hell, man, she likes you. First time she's really liked anyone since her divorce. Her ex made it big in the stock market and dumped her for a Victoria's Secret model. They live in New York, but he keeps the cabin here just to remind everyone who he is. When Dixie got the divorce papers from Danny, she walked out the door, got a job at the Purple Sage and moved in with her sister, Gracie. She let Danny have everything. Said she didn't need him or any man to make her way in this world. She was kind of living in limbo till she got it in her head to go after this reporting job, and then she stumbled onto you. And you're gay. Poor girl's got a bad streak going for her. But Dixie really is the best."

There was a glint in Jack's eyes suggesting that if Nick Romero hurt Dixie Carmichael in any way, he'd live to regret it, FBI or not.

Jack nodded toward the window. "You better get a move on. You don't know the roads well enough to be driving them in the dark."

Jack finished off his beer and left. Nick took a ten-minute shower, then climbed in the pickup and headed out of town. He'd toss the old carpet into the landfill tomorrow. For now he'd secure it under a tarp to stop remnants from flying out.

When he got to the turnoff road, it was deserted, not a soul on any of the private lanes to the incredibly huge vacation homes. The area was the perfect place to hide trucks and transfer merchandise before getting back to the expressways in no time at all.

The sign Danny's Delight came into view. Nick followed the road to a chalet nestled into the mountains, pulled up behind Dixie's Camaro and killed the engine. Quiet surrounded him. He actually heard a pinecone fall through a tree and land on the ground. Now, that was quiet.

He walked up the stone path to the big wood chalet. Nice digs. Should he knock, or should he just barge in? Perspiration dotted his upper lip and it had nothing to do with figuring out etiquette. Dixie was probably sporting some skimpy sexy see-through thing designed to drive him wild and *convert* him on the spot.

Except, he didn't need converting. He was already a true admirer of all things female, especially Dixie Carmichael. He turned the knob and pushed open the door as his eyes adjusted to the dim light. Two over-stuffed chairs, coffee table, hardwood floor, ceiling windows to the back that let in sunlight and offered a view of the woods and the mountains beyond.

A cardboard box, probably his All-Clad, sat by the sofa where Dixie lounged, wearing…*jeans and a sweatshirt!*

What the…? Where was that flimsy stuff women bought when they wanted to entice? He'd been look-ing forward to being converted and enticed, even if it only lasted a minute or two till he could tell her the truth!

She clicked on a ceramic rose lamp that sat on the end table. "We need to talk."

He didn't want to talk. He wanted to ogle, even for a few seconds, before he told her he wasn't gay. Now there was nothing to ogle except GAP across an oversized navy blue sweatshirt.

No lush curves exposed, no voluptuous breasts straining against lacy fabric or spilling over the top— damn, he liked spilling! No spicy fragrance guaran-teed to bring a man to his knees in five seconds flat.

"You broke into my place, went through my stuff. What did you think you were doing?" *Besides disappointing the hell out of me with this getup!*

"I'm trying to save you. You're a handsome man and you react to me in a sexual way no matter how much you want to deny it or you pull away. You're just confused about your masculinity, Nick, and I want to make you into the man you are. I'm going to transform you into a man's man," she growled. "I can tell that's the real Nick Romero, no matter what you say or do or what kind of accessories you buy. I have a certain sense about things and you're not who you think."

She stood and came closer. Okay, that was better. *Now* she'd take off the sweatshirt and there'd be some little skimpy thing underneath. He just wanted a harmless peek before he set her straight. Though when it involved Dixie, was anything harmless? "I'm really—"

"Bewildered. I know."

"But—"

"Trust me."

She reached behind her, but instead of removing the sweatshirt, she pulled out a bag of… "Pork rinds? You're showing me pork rinds?"

She tore off the top and plucked up one curl. "Men love these things, though I can't imagine why. Fried grease?" She put it to his mouth. "Taste. Men's food. Yum, yum. You'll get used to it."

He opened his mouth to protest and she shoved in the curl. That was okay, because he was starving and because he really did like pork rinds, especially with beer, but right now he wanted *Dixie!*

He crunched the rind and she put down the bag and grabbed a slice of cold pizza from the flat box. She wiggled the section in front of his lips. "Men can sustain life for years on this. I believe there's documented proof."

He opened his mouth to tell her he knew cold pizza was terrific—hell, he made the stuff—but she shoved the piece into his mouth. You think he'd learn to keep his mouth shut. She said, "Sort of like cardboard with tomato sauce, but with enough pepperoni I guess anything can taste good. Consider it an acquired taste. It doesn't have to be cuisine, Nick. It can be just plain food out of a box or freezer, not even homemade. Hopefully, cooked first, but sometimes not. Men don't seem to mind either way."

He said around a mouthful, "I'm not gay, Dixie."

"See!" She stepped back, beaming, spreading her arms. "This is great. I knew it, I knew it! You're getting the idea already. You're getting *the feeling*. You needed someone to point it out to you and that's me."

She aimed the wedge of bitten-off pizza at the bag of rinds on the coffee table. "Aren't these terrific foods…at least, for a guy?"

He took the slice from her fingers and put it in the

box. "No, I mean I'm *really* not gay. *Ever.* And it has nothing to do with snacks."

"That's the spirit." She punched him in the arm. "Deep down inside is a manly guy. You need to say *I am macho man* every morning when you shave. There's life beyond decorating and cooking and—"

He cupped her shoulders to hold her still—something she normally wasn't. He wanted her full attention. "My grandmother's a decorator. I've been surrounded by colors and material and rugs and pictures and sconces and the rest of that stuff all my life—well, most of it. I went to more Italian weddings than you can imagine and I had to dance. Nonna—that's Italian for *grandmother*—wouldn't have it any other way. I learned to cook because when she was out on a job it was my task to fix us dinner or make pb-and-j for myself when I was hungry. I hate peanut butter and jelly. Nonna said that if I could read, I could cook, and she's right."

"What about your mother?"

That threw him. Anything regarding his mother always did. *My mother was an alcoholic who spent more time passed out on the sofa than she ever did with her son,* he thought, but he said, "Celest raised me." And talked him into pursuing a career in the FBI instead the FBI pursuing him.

Dixie looked at Nick for a long moment, then grinned and kissed him on the cheek, her lips lingering, tantalizing him. "I understand that you're trying to explain away what you thought you were, but—"

"I like women, dammit. A lot."

"You're doing great!"

"What do you want from me, a list of references?"

She smiled patronizingly and patted his cheek. "You have things, women's things. Great women things, Nick. You have terrific taste. Men don't buy five-hundred-dollar purses. And they don't pack away pictures of Cher."

He was going to string the guys at the bureau up by their toenails. Why couldn't his last assignment be something else besides Dixie and purses and her thinking he was gay? "All those are presents for my grandmother. I knew I wouldn't be able to buy any of them in Whistlers Bend." He gazed down at her. "I am not gay, Dixie. Do you believe me? I swear that's the truth." And for once it actually was.

She bit her bottom lip. "You're thinking in the right direction, as far as I'm concerned. But I have more ways to convince you."

Here it was. What he'd imagined all the way up here. His chest tightened, making his heart pound, as she…took a pair of jeans from the sofa and held them up? Worn, a hole in the knee. She said, "You need these. Makes you look and feel kind of rugged, tough."

She draped the jeans over his shoulder, then

mussed his hair. "Doesn't it feel better to be a little messy and unkempt? And—"

He snagged her in his arms and kissed her, her full lips heaven against his. *"Dammit all,"* he finally got out. *"I am not gay!"*

He'd been doing okay, keeping his cool, till she'd run her fingers through his hair. Then he'd snapped and all his good intentions about just ogling and staying away from her vanished like the smugglers into the mountains.

He wanted her, all of her, right *now*. For a second she felt stiff, startled, shocked. Hell, he'd shocked himself! Then her body relaxed against his. She gave him a devil smile and winked. "This is really nice. But…"

"No more buts."

She smiled seductively. "What I mean is, maybe I could do with a little more convincing. I really like the way you convince. You're very good at it."

A hot ache settled below his belt. "I'm glad you think so." He brushed her lips with his, teasing her and himself, bringing them together slowly, then he deepened the kiss, his tongue touching hers for a second, and a jolt of pure ecstasy shot right through him. He coaxed her sweet lips open more, wanting to taste her again and again. She whimpered, the good kind that said she liked this as much as he did.

He splayed his hands across her back, holding her

tight, as her arms slipped around his neck, her breasts firming against his chest. Her fingers ran up his nape, setting every inch of him on fire. She brought her head back and looked at him with glazed eyes, her breathing labored and shallow. "Wow, you're a fast learner."

"I learned a long, long time ago. You happened to put two and two together and got five. I'm not a five, Dixie."

"I don't know what you're talking about." She gave him a lopsided grin and let out a bewildered sigh. "And right now I don't care."

His mouth claimed hers, making his heart jump into overdrive. "Would I be acting like a horny teenager if I was gay? You're a woman—a really delicious one, I might add—and I'm a man, which I'm sure you've noticed by now. This is pretty straightforward stuff. Don't try to complicate it. Okay?"

Her breaths came faster and she gazed into his eyes. "Either you're not gay or you're one heck of an actor. And I can't imagine why you'd fake this."

"There's not a man on the planet who'd have this reaction unless he was really attracted."

She gave him a desperate smile. "Right. I…I think I finally got it."

She swallowed. "Does this mean… Should we… Can we…" She let go of his neck and undid the top button on his shirt. When the next button refused to give way, she yanked the material apart, sending the button airborne across the room.

He laughed. "In a hurry?"

Her gaze met his. "Are you complaining?"

His erection strained against his zipper. Not only were his pants suddenly too tight, but there wasn't enough oxygen in the room and his brain fogged with lust. *What had happened to "just being friends"?*

Then she ran her fingers through his chest hair and kissed his left nipple, and the idea of *just being friends* went up in smoke along with every rational thought. He grabbed the hem of her sweatshirt and pulled it over her head, exposing her bra. A sexy see-through one, the very kind he'd thought she'd be wearing for the conversion. Having Dixie in his arms and her hands on him was all he could imagine and more. "I'm on fire for you."

She reached for his buckle and undid it, then unsnapped his jeans. He tucked his finger under her chin and brought her flushed face to his. He kissed her again, slowly, thoroughly, as her palm cupped his erection. "I'm dying here, hurry."

"Trust me, you are *so* not dead." Her hands slid inside his briefs, her cool touch on his scorched skin nearly sending him over the edge.

"Dixie," he hissed as he planted kisses along her jaw to her ear, then behind, making her shiver. His insides clenched and his remaining control waned. She stroked his hardness, held him tight, drove him insane.

"Enough." He tossed his shirt onto the couch, scooped her into his arms and laid her down. "I'd like to make this last, but—"

"Hurry." She sat up and tugged off her boots, then her jeans, leaving her in lacy panties.

"Do you always wear underwear like…this?"

She paused for a second and this time gave him a siren's smile. "Always."

"Oh, damn." He studied his boots. "Took me a half hour to put these on. What was I thinking?"

"I bet you weren't thinking this."

He sucked in air through clenched teeth, hoping for some control as she said in a desperate voice, "Nick, I don't have a half hour in me. I think I've got about a minute. Two tops. I need action! The kind you've been yakking about since you walked in the door. You do know what I'm talking about, don't you?"

Yeah, he knew all right. *"Except I can't even get my damn jeans off."*

Chapter Six

Dixie considered Nick's boots. He swallowed, his expression hungry, and not for food. She needed a quick solution. "Sit down and give me your foot."

His eyes turned midnight black. "Is this some Montana fetish you want to tell me about?"

"If the boots don't come off, your jeans don't, and neither do you and I. Get my drift? I'll pull. You'll pull. Teamwork. Think of it as…foreplay."

"I have a lot better ideas for foreplay." He sat and held out his leg.

She grabbed ahold of the boot. "Some cowboys like to wear these in bed…gives them traction." She yanked hard, fell back against the sofa arm, then tossed the boot over her head. It landed on the wood floor with a solid thud. She grabbed hold of the right foot and did the same.

He stood. "Believe me, I'm not going to have

trouble with traction. I'm not going to have trouble with anything."

He slid out of his jeans and briefs and looked down at her…at least, she thought so. She wasn't all that sure, since she was staring at *him*…a very rigid part of him.

He said, "The panties have got to go, Dix, and since you freed me of my boots, it's only fair that I remove something of yours, don't you agree?" He hooked his fingers into the thin elastic and peeled the lace over her hips, thighs, knees, then off. He let out a long sigh as she slid off her bra. "So lovely, so perfect—"

"So impatient!" She held out her arms to him and he fixed himself on top of her, his chest hairs teasing her sensitive nipples. His body felt warm and heavy and hard, and she wrapped her legs around his waist and drew him to her heat. "I want you," she breathed. "I want you so bad, Nick."

"Oh, damn!"

Her vision cleared. "If you're considering backing out now…!"

"Protection."

She put her hands over her face. "We're never going to have sex. Never. We're just going to mess around and I'm going to die from frustration."

"Then there'll be two corpses."

She unwound her legs from his back and he sat up,

straddling her hips. "You know, this is a great view. I could just sit up here and admire it."

She gave him an in-your-dreams look.

"Right. My jeans? What did I do with them?"

"Floor." She pointed down and he grabbed the denim, then took his wallet from the back pocket and pulled out the blue foil package. She said, "Going to be interesting to see that—" she pointed to his erection "—fit in that." She pointed to the flat blue square.

"Things stretch."

She bit her bottom lip. "I sure hope so. And not just the condom. You and me getting together might be a little, uh, tight." She swallowed. "The truth is, I haven't been with… I haven't done this in a long time, Nick. Like three years long. Like since Danny left me."

He arched his left eyebrow and she rushed on. "It's not that I haven't had the opportunity."

He chuckled. "Oh, I believe that. I'm just glad. Real glad." Then his lips met hers in a long kiss that curled her hair even more than that perm she'd used and sent her stomach into flips. He kissed her chin, her neck, then planted kisses to her cleavage. "I want to taste you, Dixie," he said against her heated skin. "Every delectable inch of you."

Before she could answer, his tongue stroked her left nipple, making it wet and bead, and driving the air out her lungs. He did the same to her right nipple, as her brain did a slow sizzle.

"Nick," she panted. "I thought you were…we were desperate."

"'Desperate' is vastly overrated." His voice sounded ragged. *Why wasn't he just getting on with it?*

He kissed her navel. "You smell so good. Your skin's like silk."

Her solar plexus quivered as he dropped kisses at the indent of her waist. Then his fingers teased open the soft folds between her legs and her eyes shot wide-open. "Nick?"

His tongue stroked her navel as his fingers imitated the movement. Her insides blazed, and her legs widened, letting him in deeper, making her ready for him. *Too ready!*

"Nick, I can't…"

"Let it happen, Dixie," he said, his breath hot against her belly. As his fingers stroked faster, her hips instinctively arched against him. And her body tensed in an unexpected orgasm. The room tilted…at least it felt as if it did, and her mind shattered in a million directions. How incredible! How perfect!

But she wanted him inside her, and then suddenly he was as her legs embraced him. He was so intimately a part of her now, not just physically but emotionally. She needed to make it good for him, not just take. Had a man ever treated her this way before? Never!

He thrust into her, longer, harder. Another orgasm claimed her as Nick climaxed, the moment more amazing than she had ever imagined.

His head fell beside hers, and his heavy breathing slowly returned to normal. "You are…beyond words, Dixie," he whispered in her ear.

"I feel as though this was the first time I ever made love, Nick." And in some ways it was. No man had ever put her first the way Nick had.

He finally braced himself on his elbows and gazed down at her, his lips in a half-smile. "You are an incredible lover, you know that?"

"It's you, all you."

He grinned and kissed the tip of her nose. "I'm going to clean up. You stay put." He kissed her forehead and eased himself off her. She listened to his soft footsteps on the hardwood as he made his way to the bathroom.

"Well, that turned out good," she said to herself. A smile tripped across her lips and she stifled a giggle. *Never* had she suspected she'd wind up having sex—mind-blowing sex—with Nick Romero. How could this have happened? All she'd planned on was for him to get in touch with his masculine side. Instead, he'd gotten in touch with her feminine side.

He came back and, without saying a word, pulled

on his jeans. No cuddling, no afterglow. Okay, this was not a good sign. He sat where she'd helped him with his boots. That was a worse sign. He seemed lost in thought and made a face as if he'd eaten a lemon. Her lovemaking skills were a bit rusty, but she hadn't expected *that* reaction. "What's wrong? Everything was good—or great if you happen to be me."

He rubbed his hand over his face. "I shouldn't have done this. It wasn't right."

Uh-oh! She sat up and snatched her sweatshirt from the floor, suddenly feeling vulnerable. "What happened here was a whole lot more than *right*. What happened to, 'you are beyond words, Dixie'?"

"The sex was good." He gave her a forced smile, the kind that said all hell was about to break loose. "The sex was fantastic. But, like I said when we had dinner, I really am getting over a relationship. A long one. I don't want you to be my rebound girl and that's what I'm afraid this is. I'm attracted to you. We just proved that beyond a doubt. But…."

"Rebound girl?"

"And that's not fair to you. I need time to get over—" He looked at the lamp. "Rose. We went together for years. Years and years, and I need time to adjust to life without her. To jump in the sack with you was wrong on my part. I'm sorry."

"Sorry? Jump in the sack?"

"What I mean is you deserve better than a quick roll in the hay."

"A rebound? A jump? A roll? This was nothing but a sporting event!"

He stood up, raking a hand through his hair. "The problem is I find you incredibly attractive, inside and out. You overwhelmed me, and right now I cannot be overwhelmed."

She stood up in front of him because no one *ever* looked down at Dixie Carmichael. She narrowed her eyes. "I bet if some young chickie pranced her size-two wares across this room and gave you that come-to-mama wink you'd change your ideas real fast and just love being overwhelmed. Danny sure did."

His eyes widened. "Hey, I'm not Danny."

"One Saturday morning after Danny and I made love, I strolled downstairs to start the coffee, answered the doorbell and got served with divorce papers. He lied to me, manipulated me, used me and threw me away. *'Nothing personal,'* he said. *'I just want to get on with my life without you.'* Sound familiar? Well, it's not happening again." She pointed a stiff finger at the door. "It damn well is personal. Out."

"It's not like that, Dixie. We should talk."

Talking would make a simple solution complicated. All she wanted was the jerk gone. She picked a saucepan from the box by the sofa and took aim.

He held up his hands, his eyes huge. "Not the pans!"

She flung it at the door. It hit with a hollow thump, bounced off, did a flip and fell to the floor. Okay, she felt a little better.

He looked from her to the dented pot as she grabbed the saucier. "This one I bounce off your head. Bet I'll feel a lot better after that."

"Okay, okay, I get the message. I'm going." He grabbed the saucier from her hand, then retrieved his boots and shirt and dropped them all into the box. He hoisted it into his arms and paused at the door. "I swear I don't want to hurt you. You've got to believe that, Dixie. You blow me away, and I can't have that happen right now. It's the circumstances, and these circumstances really suck. I like you, Dixie. I like you a hell of a lot more than you can imagine. But we can't get involved. Dammit. It would be a big mistake." Then he opened the door and left.

NICK PICKED HIS WAY across the dark sidewalk, muttering "Ouch, ouch, ouch" as his bare feet connected with pinecones, sticks, pebbles and everything else in the great outdoors. He deserved all the ouches and a whole lot more. If lightning struck him dead, he'd deserve that, too. Except, it was a clear night, so that was not likely to happen. *How could he have made love to Dixie when he'd known it would end in a mess?*

Because Dixie Carmichael turned him on...a lot! Mentally and physically. Making love to her was the easiest, most natural, most exciting thing he'd done in a long time.

He put the box of pans in the passenger seat of the pickup, leaned against the side of the vehicle and slid on his socks, yanked on his boots then his shirt. He climbed into the driver's side and banged his head on the steering wheel.

"Damn, damn, damn." She'd compared him to Danny, and Danny was an ass. That made Nick Romero an even bigger ass, because he'd hurt Dixie again. She suspected the reason he just wanted to be friends was that she wasn't some young, hot babe. But she was all those things. She just didn't believe it. No one deserved to be hurt once, much less twice, because she thought she was lacking in some way. Especially when the real reason was he couldn't resist her and had to keep his distance as best he could, which didn't work for crap.

He fired the engine, hit the lights and motored down the road. He needed to stay focused, and the only thing he focused on when he was with Dixie was Dixie. That didn't help in finding smugglers.

Darkness surrounded him; stars dotted the sky; moonlight faded in and out of the pines; an autumn chill swept down from the mountains. It was a perfect night to be with Dixie, wide-open windows and making love to keep warm. "Ah, hell!"

He skidded around a turn that seemed to head up. He didn't remember the turn being that sharp, and wasn't he supposed to be going down? He took another hairpin turn and zeroed in on a big— "Buffalo! Holy crap!"

Nick hit the brakes and swerved onto the widened shoulder of the road. The truck skidded through a cluster of pines, then nosedived over the edge and bounced across rocks into a ditch before stopping dead against a tree trunk. The airbag exploded, flattening him to the back of the seat, then deflated. "Piss-poor ending to a really piss-poor day." Then he remembered making love to Dixie. Not everything had been piss-poor.

He swiped the airbag from his lap, took his cell phone from the glove compartment, pressed it on, but got no reception. *Big surprise there.* He couldn't even call Wes to come help. 'Course he'd laugh his butt off over Nick meeting up with a buffalo, but at least he'd help pull Nick back on the road.

He rummaged through the glove compartment, located a flashlight and shoved open the truck door. He might be able to get out by himself. The old carpet in the truck bed added weight, providing more traction. That was the second time tonight that the word had been used. Hadn't Dixie said something about traction and boots and *sex?* He couldn't get his mind off her, even in a ditch in the middle of flipping nowhere.

He had pulled off a piece of old carpet and was

wedging it under the back wheels, when he heard the deep hum of one motor, then two. Trucks. And they were slowing down, pulling behind the trees he'd just cut through.

Nick doused the flashlight, then his vehicle's headlights. Could be kids out for a joyride or a necking party. Except this road didn't offer squat in the way of joy or a good ride and kids didn't need to venture into the mountains to find a necking spot around here. And the motors weren't like those of the pickups the kids around here drove. They were bigger, had more horsepower.

The trucks stopped, their motors idling, and Nick could see headlights at the edge. A man came into view. Tall, barrel chest, broad-shouldered. He said in a Texas twang, "You sure this is right? Maybe we're lost. There's nothing here."

"That's the whole point," a younger voice replied as he walked into the beams. He was shorter, leaner, with a baseball cap on backward. He continued, "I checked the mileage when we exited the expressway. This is where we meet Theo. He'll be a few minutes behind us so we don't attract attention like a convoy coming up here."

Another motor sounded in the distance, a bigger truck going slow. "See?" the younger man said. "We're right where we should be. We'll make a killing this time."

Another young voice chimed in. "We'll reach Chicago in two days if we drive straight through, then on to Cleveland. Got vendors ready and waiting for us. We get back here in five days and keep it up till the snow hits and we have to move south. I'm getting a bigger truck. Man, this is easy money. Where are you headed?"

"St. Louis and Nashville," said another older voice. "Anyone ever tell you guys you talk too damn much?"

The bigger motor stopped and the men left the side of the road. Nick swore. He was outmanned and outgunned. All he had was a Glock taped under his seat in the truck. He wasn't taking anyone down tonight and he had to keep quiet. If these guys suspected the FBI was onto them, they'd change routes and all the leads would be lost.

He couldn't hear over the rumble of the motors. An owl hooted nearby, something furry scurried in the bushes and the breeze dropped the temperature a few more degrees. Damn, he wanted to look over that rise, but if he snapped a twig or lost his footing, he was dead meat…literally.

Finally, truck doors slammed and one engine faded. A few minutes later the other trucks followed. Nick scurried to the top and peered over the side, hoping to get a license number, but it was too dark. The only thing he could make out was the back end of a white delivery truck heading out of the pines. He pulled himself onto the road, and as he did, he tripped over a small paper bag. He picked it up. It was blue, with Tiffany & Co. printed on the front in white. He stuffed the bag in his back pocket and checked his watch. The whole transfer had taken twenty-five minutes. Those guys had offloading the merchandise down to a science, and they'd be back in five days. Now he had to figure out where they'd meet up next time.

He stood on the road, and looked around. Nothing but tire tracks caught his attention till another motor sounded, coming his way up the hillside. A car this time. The place was Grand Central Station!

Nick jumped behind a stand of pines. Headlights illuminated the road as the car swung around the curve. Dixie's Camaro. Sports cars were not the vehicle of choice for this terrain. He walked out from his hiding place, waving his arms. He really didn't want her to see him because that would bring on a barrage of questions, but Dixie shouldn't be out here alone with smugglers on the loose. Why hadn't she stayed in the damn cabin, where she was safe? Never did he suspect that she'd go out driving in the middle of the night. And that was damn stupid of him.

She stopped and lowered the window. He poked his head inside, her unique womanly scent wrapping around him like a familiar warm blanket. Her eyes were bright and brazen as he said, "What are you do-ing here?"

She tossed her head in a sassy way that irritated him no end. Whatever he said would not matter one damn bit. She was a reporter on a mission; the story was the thing—the only thing. "Not that it's any of your business, but I'm out hunting for smugglers. I got a feeling they're up here somewhere. Full moon, deserted roads, close to expressways. Works for me."

The woman not only turned him on but turned every hair in his head gray. "You could be walking into a lot more trouble than you can imagine. Go back to town and read a book or something."

She gave him a sweet smile and batted her big eyes. "Drop dead, Romero. You're not telling me what to do. You might be more comfortable in your kitchen with your pots and pans, but that's not where I want to be. I've got a big story to write." Her eyebrows drew together. "Why are you up here, anyhow? This isn't the way back to town. Where's your pickup?"

Well, this was damn embarrassing. He nodded to-ward the side of the road, where her headlights were aimed. "Pickup's over there. I sort of…slid. Took the wrong turn from the chalet and wound up here."

"Wrong turn? The road goes up the mountain and down. What's to get wrong?"

Everything. He couldn't think straight with Dixie on his mind and this proved it beyond a doubt.

"You're lucky you didn't do worse than slide. There are some nasty cliffs. I should give you pointers on driving in the mountains."

"Gee, thanks, but driving's a little tricky when there's a buffalo on the road."

Her eyes went as big as the stars overhead and she sat straight up. "Buffalo?"

"I guess that's what it was. Can't be sure. My knowledge on the subject is limited to old nickels and the nature channel."

"Ohmygosh!" She flung open the car door, making him jump aside. She glanced around as though gold was hidden behind every tree. "Where'd you see him? This way, that way? I wonder if it's Andy."

"I swerved—he ran. We didn't exchange names." Nick hitched his thumb over the side of the drop-off. "Bet I'm not insured for buffalo encounters. And why is this buffalo so important that he has a name?"

Dixie leaned against the car hood. "Andy is Maggie's buffalo, missing for two months now. He's her stud-muffin for starting her beefalo herd, some new kind of cattle thing that's suited for smaller ranches. Anyway, Andy got buffalo-rustled. He escaped and has been running footloose ever since—seems to be enjoying himself to no end."

She went to the edge of the road and peered over. Nick joined her there, and the two of them looked down the hill to the pickup. The only sound was the breeze in the trees; the only light came from the Camaro. Why couldn't he be out here with Dixie just taking a walk, his arm around her, counting stars, pointing out constellations, talking about the town and the people?

He bent forward to get a better idea how he'd have to maneuver the car to get it out, when Dixie pulled something from his back pocket. "What's this?"

Oh, hell! He'd been saying that a lot since Dixie had barged into his life. "It's a bag I found."

"I saw a corner sticking out. No mistaking a robin's egg blue bag like this." She held it up to his flashlight. "Where'd you get a Tiffany bag?"

"Up on the road. I was going to give it to you. Guess I forgot." Okay, how did she do it? Find clues like this, even when they were stuffed in his pocket.

"Are you kidding? Not every day one of these winds up on a mountain road." She smiled, her teeth white against the darkness. "You know what this means—the smugglers were here. Much easier to sell Tiffany knockoffs if you can pack them in the proper knockoff bag."

She studied it. "And from its condition, the smugglers were here recently…very recently. No watermarks or dirt splashed from the rain. It's not even dusty. Did you see anything besides Andy? Trucks coming and going?"

"Only Andy and me and the trip down the mountain." She must have missed passing those truckers by a few minutes. Thank God for that! What if she'd followed them? The situation was getting too dangerous.

"This is some find," she said with way too much enthusiasm in her voice. She walked back to the Camaro and called over her shoulder, "I'll move my car over and light up the area so you can see how to back your truck out."

He wanted that bag, dammit. And he wanted to kiss her. Hard to tell which he wanted more. He maneuvered his way down the hill, tripping over rocks, trying not to slip on leaves and grass. Why did Dixie have to be so closely connected to this assignment? Why did she have to be a reporter? Why couldn't she be content as a waitress at the Sage? Life would be so much easier. Hell, life was never easy.

He climbed into the truck cab and turned the ignition. At least he wasn't spending the night in the woods. And Dixie was talking to him…sort of. The engine hummed. He shifted into Reverse and hit the gas. The tires spun, grabbed the carpet, and the truck ground its way back onto the road. He got out and surveyed the damage.

"I think you need a new bumper and grill," Dixie said.

What he needed was to have his head examined for being attracted to the biggest busybody in town. He flipped up the collar of her jacket against the breeze, surprising her just as he'd intended, using the oldest trick in the book to get what he wanted. Create a diversion one place; take what you need from another. "Thanks for helping me tonight."

"Don't read too much into it. I'm still angry with you. Besides, I owe you for finding the bag. Consider my help payback."

Except she didn't need to pay him back at all, since he'd just lifted the bag from her pocket. He didn't want her flashing it around, making the smugglers even more aware than they already were that she was on their trail. They had connections in the area; he felt sure of that. How else would they have known to look for Drew in Whistlers Bend and not some ranch or farm or even in Rocky Fork?

"Follow me down the mountain," Dixie said. "It's easier that way."

A gust of wind played with her red curls and he itched to do the same. "Right."

He got into the truck and waited till she turned around. With luck, Dixie would think she'd dropped the bag or misplaced it. With no luck, she'd suspect him of taking it. And this was the second time he'd swiped evidence from her. The bag, the card, Wes, the designer paraphernalia—how long before she put them all together? In a small town, information about what she'd found would leak out in no time. He needed more lies, more diversions to lead Dixie in another direction.

One of these days he'd make it up to her. He'd level with her and tell her why he'd done what he had. Then he'd apologize for feeding her the "let's be friends" line, because that was the biggest lie of all. He didn't just want to be friends with Dixie. He wanted a lot more.

DIXIE YAWNED as the breakfast crowd at the Sage waned. She refilled coffee cups with one hand and served the Hungry Heifer special to Gracie's ex, refraining from dumping the contents into his lap. Not that Glen didn't deserve it. He never paid for his breakfast when he stopped in at the Sage because he knew Dixie wouldn't turn in the father of her adorable niece and nephew. That rat.

Dixie laughed and joked with two cowboys and sashayed as usual, but her head and her heart were somewhere else…like with Nick "Jerk-extraordinaire" Romero! Could she and Gracie pick men or what! They needed to write a book: *Twelve Easy Steps to the Relationships from Hell.*

How could she have slept with him? How could she have jumped so willingly into his bed…or, more accurately, onto Danny's leather couch? Lois Lane wouldn't have jumped. Then again, she'd fallen for a guy who wore his underwear on the outside and changed in phone booths.

"Hey," Maggie said as she parked herself at their

table. "How'd the great rescue mission go? I drove all the way in from the ranch to find out."

"You drove in to town to see Jack and we both know it."

"There is that. He has a meeting. So, now that I'm here, what happened? Did the conversion work?"

The few remaining customers were okay for a moment, so Dixie could talk. She sat down across from to Maggie. "The good news is your buffalo's in the mountains, not far from your ranch. The other good news is Nick Romero's not gay."

Maggie grinned. "Well, that's great, except you don't look like you agree."

"Nick not being gay was good news for about twenty minutes, then he said again that he thought being friends was a good idea."

Maggie glared. "But if he's not gay, why does he have the designer stuff?"

"Presents for his grandmother, who lives in Italy, which makes no sense, since that's a fashion and designer Mecca." Dixie sighed. "Last night Nick's car went off the road and I helped him get it out of a ditch. There were big tire tracks on the pull-off that weren't run over by his pickup—meaning he was there first. And—here's where it gets really interesting—he had a knockoff Tiffany bag in his pocket, which I took from him and he somehow stole back. Twice now he's taken my evidence."

"And this all leads to…"

"Somehow, someway, Nick is in with the smugglers." She put her hands over her face. "First I fell for a gay guy, now a crook."

"You've really fallen for him?"

"Maybe, a little. But I'm getting over it…I think."

"You're wrong on this, Dix. Jack contacted Denver, had Nick checked out. He's just a chef, credentials and all."

"That's what makes Nick the perfect cover. No record, squeaky clean. Not a badass bone in his body. No tattoos or muscle shirt or bad teeth. No reason to suspect he had any connection to anything illegal."

"Totally namby-pamby?"

"Well, most of the time." She thought about their making love and there was nothing namby-pamby about that. "But I've got a plan. I'm going to be his friend, all right. Fact is, I'm going to stick to that no-good sidewinder like glue, and then I'll let him lead me to the smugglers. I can get my story and fry his butt both at the same time! That double-crosser."

She nodded at the entrance to the Sage. "And I can start now because the dear man's at the door with a bouquet of flowers the size of Andy. Too bad Mr. Romero doesn't realize they're for his own funeral."

Chapter Seven

Nick paused in the doorway of the Purple Sage, everyone taking in the flowers he held and him mostly hidden behind them. He had to do this. Not just to drive home the image that he was nothing but a milquetoast chef and to make peace with Dixie so she'd let him in on whatever she found out about the smugglers, but because he was sorry for a lot of things. He couldn't confess all now, but with the flowers she'd understand that he cared—at least, he hoped so.

She looked great today. Hell, she looked great every day. Would he ever tire of her curls, her smile that was actually closer to a grin, her relentless energy and how she threw herself into whatever she believed in? Never.

He wound his way through the sparsely occupied tables and stopped in front of Dixie. Maggie stood. "I have to go. There's been a buffalo encounter that

Get FREE BOOKS and a FREE GIFT when you play the...

LAS VEGAS

GAME

Just scratch off the gold box with a coin. Then check below to see the gifts you get!

YES! I have scratched off the gold box. Please send me my **2 FREE BOOKS** and **gift for which I qualify**. I understand that I am under no obligation to purchase any books as explained on the back of this card.

354 HDL D7ZM   **154 HDL D7XP**

FIRST NAME	LAST NAME

ADDRESS

APT.#	CITY

(H-AR-12/05)

STATE/PROV.   ZIP/POSTAL CODE

www.eHarlequin.com

7	7	7	Worth TWO FREE BOOKS plus a BONUS Mystery Gift!
🍒	🍒	🍒	Worth TWO FREE BOOKS!
🔔	🔔	🍀	TRY AGAIN!

The Harlequin Reader Service® — Here's how it works:

If offer card is missing write to: Harlequin Reader Service, 3010 Walden Ave., P.O. Box 1867, Buffalo NY 14240-1867

BUSINESS REPLY MAIL
FIRST-CLASS MAIL   PERMIT NO. 717-003   BUFFALO, NY

POSTAGE WILL BE PAID BY ADDRESSEE

HARLEQUIN READER SERVICE
3010 WALDEN AVE
PO BOX 1867
BUFFALO NY 14240-9952

NO POSTAGE
NECESSARY
IF MAILED
IN THE
UNITED STATES

requires my attention." She smiled at Nick. "Nice flowers."

Maggie left and he handed Dixie the bouquet. "Sorry if I offended you in any way last night, and thanks for directing me out of that ditch."

She put the array on the table, then kissed him on the cheek. Okay, that reaction was better than he'd hoped for, except it didn't fit. Where was the beady-eyed look that said *It's going to take a lot more than a roomful of posies to get me to even glance your way again, buster?* Now, that was the Dixie he knew. The real Dixie. This Dixie… What the hell was she up to now? Only one way to find out: get her talking. "How about another picnic? My treat this time, since our last one got rained out."

Her eyes brightened. "That's a great idea. Pick any place that interests you."

"I'm new here. You decide."

"Your turn. You drive. We'll jump in your slightly dented truck and go where the road takes us. Can you pick me up around two at Gracie's? Second white frame on Bolder Street. I need to drop off my story at the *Whistle Stop* before we go. It's about what happens when the only beauty salon in town closes."

Nick grinned. "Guess I should duck for cover."

"It's not that kind of story. In fact, you'll like it. Gracie's opening a salon. Converting her basement. My story's about one business closing and another starting up to fill the void. Now I just have to get Mr. Eversole to go for it. If a story doesn't have to do with cattle or mining, he's not interested. The *Whistle Stop* is so stuck in the fifties. After I drop off the article, I have to help Gracie move stuff around in the basement so she can start on the salon, and then we can go."

"No sense in two women doing all that lugging. Wes is in town taking pictures." He really was there so the two of them could meet Jack and plan what to do about the smugglers, but this would work, too. "He'd be glad to help Gracie. She can have all the stuff in the shed at my place. Wes can move it and we can get an earlier start."

Dixie tipped her head. "You're giving Gracie all those salon things?"

She flashed him one of those smiles that touched his heart and made him hate himself all the more for constantly lying to her. "She can cut my hair for free and we'll call it even."

He made for the door and she called to him, "Thanks for the flowers, Nick Romero."

He left the diner. Dixie's forgiveness had come way too easy. He'd expected it could take days to get her to talk to him again, and here she was, joining him on a picnic. No groveling necessary. It didn't feel right. It didn't feel like Dixie.

He headed for his place to meet up with Jack and Wes. He wanted to show them the Tiffany bag and see if they'd heard anything new about the operation. He unlocked the front door to his place and went in. The new tiles and buckets of stucco were piled in the corner. The place would look great. Noises came from the kitchen, so he headed there, past the unpacked boxes of new china, wineglasses and utensils sitting against the wall. Everything very restaurantlike, keeping his cover legit for right now to satisfy nosy neighbors, and, all going with him when he left Whistlers Bend. The bureau should give him a gold star for footing the bill for all this. Then again, he would use everything later.

Jack and Wes sat at the kitchen table, chowing down on leftover ziti and drinking his beer. "Just make yourselves at home."

"We did," Wes said around a mouthful. "Damn, it's great having a partner who can cook. You are the bomb in the kitchen, man."

Jack held up a forkful of pasta in agreement, his mouth too full to talk. Nick pulled out a chair and sat on it backward. He put his hand on Wes's shoulder. "And *you're* just the man I want to see."

Wes swallowed and grinned. "Take another truck off the road and need me to help out?"

Nick laughed. His no-secrets theory was right on the money. "Only if I meet up with the missing local buffalo again. The best part is a buffalo wasn't the only thing I ran into on that mountain. The smugglers showed, using a pull-off behind a stand of pines where I slid off the road."

Both men stopped eating and Jack said, "I'll be damned. That's the closest anyone's gotten to them so far."

"It wasn't my choice. I was in the ditch and they didn't know I was around. I heard them say they'd be coming back for another shipment in five days. That gives us four days to figure out where they'll meet up. I've convinced Dixie to go on another picnic. We'll go east of the depot. Maybe we'll come across something that will help us narrow the places to stake out. She's so damn lucky at stumbling across clues it's frightening. Though I found this on my own." He snagged the blue bag from his pocket and tossed it into the middle of the table. "Our smugglers are getting sloppy. A good sign."

"I'll scout around west of the depot where you went off the road," Jack said.

"What am I chopped liver?" Wes asked.

Nick grinned. "No, you're the moving man. You're going to help Dixie's sister rearrange her basement. I volunteered you."

Wes stabbed a meatball. "*This* is why I joined the FBI?"

"It's the only way I could get Dixie out of the house with me now. We've got to start pulling this operation together. We're running out of time."

Nick made for the new Sub-Zero fridge to get stuff for sandwiches and salad.

Wes wolfed down the last of the pasta and Jack finished his beer, then stood. "Let me know if you find anything on your picnic. We'll keep at this until we turn up some information. Like you said, we have four days. At least we know they'll be back here then."

Wes and Jack left, and Nick put together the lunch, adding a bottle of "Le More" from the Castelluccio Estates, where Celest lived. He and Dixie were all about business from here on out. No fooling around, no more chalet encounters. But he did have her to himself for an afternoon, and there was no reason not to enjoy Dixie as much as he could from afar. Except he hated afar. He wanted her close and he really wanted to make love to her again.

DIXIE EYED Nick's pickup idling in the driveway. It looked a little scratched up, but not too bad. She grabbed her duffel and lugged it outside. He met her halfway up the brick walk and took the bag, the pans clattering. "What the hell is this? You're hauling pans two days in row?"

Nick Romero was, without a doubt, the most handsome man God had put on earth, she thought as he added, "I brought lunch." He rattled the pans, his eyes narrowing, a smile spreading across his lips. "You don't have to cook."

"The only way Eversole would print my story on Gracie's salon and your restaurant was if I did a piece on mining. So, we're going to pan for gold and you're holding our equipment."

And she'd so rather be holding his equipment, instead of just standing there talking to him. They'd been together less than five minutes and this was where her mind was already! What would happen after a couple of hours? This was no way to start a friendly picnic. *Think friendly, friendly, friendly—not sex, sex, sex,* she ordered herself.

He hoisted the pans into the truck bed, his muscles tightening under his T-shirt, pulling across his firm abs, making her crazy for him. She climbed into the cab, and he got in beside her and fired the engine. "Ready?"

Oh, she was so ready. Ready to jump his bones right there in the truck. The afternoon was going to be a long one. Hopefully, Nick would let some smuggling information slip out and her present case of sexual frustration would be worth it.

He backed out of the drive, careful to miss Kate's tricycle and Cameron's bicycle with training wheels, and headed down the street. His male scent filled the truck—at least, her side—and she couldn't take her eyes from him.

"What are you after?" Nick asked.

She froze in her seat and stared at him. "Excuse me?"

"What do you hope to find…on our picnic?" He gave her a glance. "And you're blushing."

"Sunburn." *More like Nick-burn!* "Where should we picnic?"

"Someplace with water. Panning for gold is tough without it. Any ideas?"

His gaze fused with hers for a moment, his eyes as black as the Montana sky at midnight. She swallowed. *Holy cannoli!* He was thinking about her in the same way she was thinking about him. How could she want to have sex with a smuggler, especially one who'd slept with her, then left her? Lust had no common sense!

They needed a distraction right now. "Take the road to the depot. Remember that lake I mentioned the other day, the one with good fishing by the old railroad tracks? We can picnic there. Pan for gold flakes." And if she stood in the cold water, that was sure to zap her back into sanity.

"So, we really are going to pan for gold?"

"If I want my article in the *Whistle Stop* we are. I'll get pictures of you. That'll be good for your business. A lot of people camp and pan on the weekends for fun. Eversole is a real pro. Even leads expeditions into the mountains. He's got gold fever bad. He spends more time being a miner than an editor. The pictures and the story will make you look like you're fitting in. It's important to do that, isn't it?" She studied him for a minute, waiting for a reaction. "Fit in, I mean."

"As you said, it's good for business."

The smuggling business. He comes and blends right in and no one suspects who he really is. He rounded the bend, with the lake to the side, mountains in the background. "This is incredible," Nick said as he drew to a stop. "Who owns all this?"

"It's a state park."

"Good. The idea of it turning into a strip mall gives me the creeps. I've had enough of the city, the big life, the action. This is what I want now. And you want just the opposite."

She sat sideways and faced him. "Aren't you afraid you'll die of boredom?"

"I sure hope so." He tucked a strand of hair behind her ear, the simple touch an intimate connection she hadn't counted on. He continued. "Though when you're around, I can't imagine being bored."

He looked as though he wanted to kiss her and she sure wanted to kiss him. She swallowed a whine and scrounged up some self-control. "We should get going."

She climbed from the truck and hauled the picnic basket and her camera from the back. Nick got the panning supplies. "Where'd you get these, anyway? You do a lot of panning?"

Dixie started down to the lake and he followed, the pans clanking along. "They belong to Glen, Gracie's ex. Getting rich quick is his life's ambition. He convinced Gracie they should get a second mortgage on the house and fix it up. He took the money, their savings and left her with the kids. Lost the whole she-bang in Vegas. I saw him this morning at the Sage. Sure hope he stays away from Gracie and the kids." She stopped at an even spot of grass that dipped into the lake. "This okay?"

"This is paradise." Then he looked back at her, his eyes even darker, and she knew he included her in that statement. Trouble was she felt the same way. Not good! No getting it on with the local smuggler!

"Let's pan first," she suggested.

"Aren't you famished?"

"You have no idea." She froze. He swallowed. Then she swallowed. "Oh, damn. Did I just say that?"

"I think you did."

"Maybe we should go."

"You have the panning story to do. We…we'll be fine. Friends, remember? Nothing more."

"Right." She forced a smile. "I'll give you friendly lessons on panning." She slung her camera strap over her shoulder, hitching it high to keep it dry. She snagged a pan. "Follow me." They trooped to edge of the lake. "Dip the pan in the water to collect some gravel, swill the gravel around to drain out the water. The gold sinks to the bottom. Piece of cake."

He hunkered down beside her to watch. He was too close, too handsome, and she wanted him way too much. She thrust the pan his way and got tweezers and a little bottle from her pocket. "Pluck out the gold flecks. Save them in the bottle. When you get enough, you can sell your findings. I don't keep track of what gold's going for an ounce right now. Panning's fun. You can even afford a beer from your findings once in a while."

But she'd much rather be having fun with Nick than talking gold. She stood. She was rambling, and she was way too turned on for friendship. She had to get away from him. "Your turn."

He dipped the pan and repeated what she'd done, as she snapped pictures. He photographed well. Green grass, blue water, Nick's dark features, Nick naked. She had to get out of here. "I'll see if there's a better place to pan."

She walked away. She could feel him staring at her, but she couldn't look at him or she'd go back. She needed to cool off. Like that was ever going to happen. She could walk from here to the moon and still want that man.

What to do? He was so handsome and kind and compassionate…and a crook! She turned back for another peck and saw a bear eating at the picnic basket, Nick with his back to the scene as he panned away, oblivious. Holy crap! She knew better than to leave food out. How dumb on her part. What had she done? Her brain was total mush.

She slowly retraced her steps. Moving fast was not a good idea with a bear. She had pepper spray, but it was with the panning supplies. Besides, some people thought bears considered pepper spray a condiment to the main meal. Just then, Nick glanced up, his eyes connecting with hers. She made a quiet sound with her finger across her lips and pointed to the bear. Nick cut his eyes to the bear and stopped dead. Thank heavens he didn't run.

The bear sat on the blanket and gobbled food from one crockery container, then another. Dixie snapped pictures of Nick, the bear and the surrounding debris. This could be a neat story if they lived long enough for her to write it.

Finally, the bear finished, stood—did he just burp?—and waddled toward Nick. Dixie's heart jumped to her throat and she bit hard on her bottom lip. Bear attacks were more rare than lightning strikes, but they did happen.

The bear burped again, stopped and meandered into the woods. Once he was there, Dixie walked up beside Nick and surveyed the damage. "I think he gave you a five-paw rating."

"From the way he took off for the woods, I don't think the Dijon dressing on the pasta salad agreed with his digestive tract."

"For which we are eternally grateful. You could have been dessert." She stood on tiptoes and kissed him on the mouth. She couldn't let another minute pass without doing that. What if he'd been hurt? He might be a smuggler, but…but… Darn, she really liked him anyway. Wasn't she supposed to have more sense at forty? When did all that wisdom-coming-with-age stuff kick in? Now. Now!

He wrapped his arms around her, the heat from his body mixing with hers. A perfect time, a perfect place, an almost perfect man. Did he have to be almost?

His hands slid under her T-shirt, the feel of his fingers on her bare skin turning her on even more. Except this was so, so wrong. Falling for Nick set her up for a ton of heartache. Danny had left her for the model; Nick would leave her for prison. Danny had gotten the better deal, but leaving was leaving.

She stepped back. "I can't do this again. Splitting up is tough."

"I didn't realize we were together."

"Yeah, well, we're headed that way—at least for now—and then it's going to get complicated and all fall apart because—" *because you are in such deep doo-doo and going to jail* "—because I'm leaving the Bend."

He started picking up the discarded pots. "What about the panning story?"

"I got some shots, and the bear incident here will really make a good story. People love those almost-eaten-by-a-bear stories."

"Thank heaven for the almost." He winked. She laughed and so did he, the tension between them broken, sort of. The friendship thing worked. They got along and could talk. Of course, friends also leveled with each other, and Nick was light-years away from doing that.

He retrieved the panning equipment and loaded it into the truck. She followed with the basket. "No evidence of the smugglers being here," she volunteered as he climbed into the cab and caught the engine.

"This place is too out in the open—no place to hide." He'd responded immediately, as if he understood exactly where smugglers would hang out and where they wouldn't. He was so in with them. She couldn't think of much to say on the way back except *Turn yourself in to the authorities and beg for mercy.* That wasn't going to happen and she had no idea what to do about it except…turn him in? Oh, heck! Could she really do that?

Nick pulled into Gracie's driveway behind Wes's Jeep. She had to say something. *Thanks for a great picnic?* That didn't work. "I bet Wes and Gracie have that basement all ready for wallboard and paint. Let's go see. Gracie's kids are spending the day at a friend's house so she can fix the salon. Nice of Wes to help out. We're back early." Gads, she was rambling again.

Nick grabbed the duffel. "Where do you store the panning equipment?"

They'd deteriorated to small talk. She hated small talk as much as she hated rambling. "Panning equipment goes in the garage around back. I'll go check on renovations."

She walked to the house, then took the outside entrance to the basement. The door was painted bright yellow now, and had a little Wet Paint sign hanging from the knob. Carefully, she opened the door—to hair-washing bowls stacked in one corner, some counters and cabinets, mirrors leaning against the walls and three white swivel chairs in the middle of the floor. Wes sat in one and Gracie sat in his lap, and they were sharing a kiss to end all kisses.

Gracie's hands in Wes's shirt; his hands under her blouse; tongues engaged in some wild mating dance—least, that's what it looked like. Wes's eyes rounded as he caught sight of her, and Gracie turned her way, startled but not budging. She grinned and finger-waved to Dixie. "Hi, sister dear."

Wes reddened from the neck up. "You're back early."

Dixie swallowed. "Sorry. I didn't realize you…"

"We didn't, either," Gracie said, her cheeks pinking as she slid from Wes's lap and straightened her shirt. "It…we…this just kind of happened."

She held out her hand to Wes. He took it and stood, sliding his arm around Gracie's waist in a protective fashion as she added, "And I'm not sorry it did."

Wes did the dopey smile. "Me, too."

If Nick was a smuggler, so was Wes. Oh, terrific! The Carmichael sisters weren't having any better luck with this second round of men in their lives than they had with Glen and Danny.

NICK LUGGED the panning equipment down the driveway past the house to the detached garage. He opened the side door and set the duffel on a storage rack in the corner behind a blue Honda Civic. He started back down the drive, and spotted someone in Gracie's house. A man, head down, tearing through the place, obviously searching for something, obviously not supposed to be there, obviously not Wes.

Nick ducked below the windows, found the back door to the house and let himself in. He crept to the back room, came up behind the man and took him in a chokehold. "Looking for something, buddy?"

The guy gasped. "Who the hell are you?"

"Concerned citizen. If you belonged here, you wouldn't be sneaking around when everyone else is downstairs, and you wouldn't be tearing hell out of the place."

"My house. I got a right."

Nick let the man go and stepped back. "Glen."

He flashed a sly grin. "Guess I got a reputation."

"As a no-good jerk who takes money from his

wife and kids. That's what you were doing here now. Seems to be your m.o."

"And you're that new cook in here from Denver." Glen rubbed his neck, sizing Nick up. "Cook, my ass. They don't teach those holds in no cooking school. Who the hell are you really?"

"The man who's going to kick your butt so hard you won't sit down for a month if you ever show up here again. Got it?"

Glen's eyes narrowed; his lips curled. "You and what army, pretty boy?"

"Trust me, I got the army and I'm not pretty when I'm pissed, and you're pissing me off big-time. Get the hell out of here and don't stop trucking till you pass the Montana state line. I got friends and they have friends. Don't come back."

Glen gave Nick a cold stare, then left. Nick headed for the basement. He'd tell Gracie and Dixie about Glen, and he'd tell Wes and Jack. They all needed to keep an eye out. Two women living alone with two kids and Glen the scum ball visiting wasn't a good mix.

Nick passed through the tidy ranch-style house and found the stairs. He started down and met Dixie coming up. Something was wrong. "You look…upset."

"What are you doing up here?"

"Later. Didn't Wes and Gracie get along? You look like something happened. What?"

"Oh, Wes and Gracie got along, all right. Real

well. Too well. There's something about the Carmichael women that attracts all the wrong kind of men."

"Hey, Wes is a great guy, and somehow I'm mixed up in that crack, too."

She sighed. "You think so, Nick? Just maybe?"

All the fight and sarcasm went out of her. She let out a deep breath and rested her forehead against his chin. "Damn you, Nick Romero. Damn you, damn you, damn you." Then she walked out the door.

Okay, what the hell was that all about? Something to do with Wes and Gracie? And him? Before he could go down the stairs, Wes came up and asked, "Is Dixie okay?"

"No. What went wrong?"

Wes blushed and Nick said, "Hell, man, what did you do?"

"Nothing…yet. Gracie and I sort of clicked and Dixie walked in on us fooling around." He shrugged. "We weren't fooling around, fooling around, but damn close. I wasn't expecting you for a while. Dixie suddenly got all upset, and now Gracie's all upset."

"You and Gracie?"

"Maybe, but Gracie's really worried about her sister."

"Let me get to the bottom of this. Oh, and tell Gracie to start locking her doors and to keep an eye out. Her creep of an ex was here going through her things, digging for money."

Wes's eyes widened a fraction and turned steely. No one would have noticed except Nick. They knew each other the way they knew themselves. *Mother* was pissed. And *Mother* cared about Gracie.

"Think I'll hang around here for a while," Wes said. "The kids should be home soon."

"Watch your back, and everyone else's."

"Always," Wes said.

Nick gave a quick nod and left. He had to find Dixie. What was going on with her? Something with him and her, and now Wes, and now Gracie.

What the hell could it be?

Chapter Eight

Nick backed his truck out of Gracie's driveway and headed for the Purple Sage. Maybe Dixie had gone there. Something had her ready to spit nails, and he wanted to know what. He cared more than he should on a case, but there wasn't much he could do about how he felt. The point was not to act on his feelings, to keep a clear head and do the assignment. He parked the truck at the curb and went inside; the place filling up for dinner. No Dixie.

When he came out, Jack drove by in his cruiser, and Nick flagged him down. Another man was in the car. Big, military hair, olive T-shirt. Army? "Have you seen Dixie?" Nick asked.

Jack nodded down the street. "She's marking out the route for that 5-K run she's got planned. How'd it go today? You and Dixie find anything at the lake?"

"A bear." And a ton of frustration. He cut his eyes

to the army man and Jack said, "Meet Flynn MacIntire, army colonel. His boy found the Louis Vuitton. We keep Flynn in the loop because he's mean and ugly. He also just got back from adopting a baby from Central America." Nick grinned and shook hands with Flynn. Jack continued. "I looked around the area where you went off the road. I doubt if the smugglers will meet up there again. But we have no clue where else they'll meet."

"And they're headed back here in two days if my estimate is right about there being a five-day lapse between meetings," Nick said. "We better come up with something. Plus there's another wrinkle. Dixie might be onto me. She's acting weird. Wes's cover and mine won't last much longer, no matter how much restaurant equipment I order."

"We'll meet at the office at seven. Figure out the most likely spots the smugglers will be. We'll need to cover as much of the area as possible by ourselves. If we use too many outsiders, we'll spook the bad guys. I'd bet anything they have a snitch in town."

"Keep an eye out at Gracie's. I caught her ex rifling through her house. Wes is there now."

Jack grinned. "I heard. Seems we got a new romance in town."

Nick chuckled. "This just happened about an hour ago."

"Yeah, the gossips are slipping," Jack said. "We usually get faster feedback. Good luck with Dixie, and I mean that more ways than one."

The cruiser took off and Nick drove down the street, passing the food market on the way. Barney had come out to lock up for the day. Nick stopped to say hi and Barney said, "If you're looking for Dixie, she's headed for the movie house. Just bought a pedometer to walk off the route for that breast cancer event." He stood up tall. "I'm entering, doing the 5-K run. Been training since Dixie wrote that piece about it in the *Whistle Stop*."

Nick leaned against the side of the building as Barney secured the front doors. "Why do you think I'm searching for Dixie? I could be out taking an evening drive."

"Not with that look in your eyes. You got a woman on your mind, boy, and we're all willing to bet it's Dixie. I put some nice tomatoes, squash and a yellow pepper in back for you. Stop by tomorrow morning and pick them up. Good luck with Dixie. You two go well together."

Nick watched Barney mosey down the sidewalk to his house on Laurel. His wife, Ruth, probably had dinner waiting, and then they'd take a stroll down by the lake. He knew the people in Whistlers Bend and they knew him and trusted him. What would their reaction be when they found out he'd deceived them all this time? Not good, and that was a damn shame. He liked it here a lot.

Nick parked the truck and walked toward the movie house. The marquee lights overhead illuminated—a Cary Grant festival this week. *Charade* played tonight. The scent of fresh popcorn wafted out onto the sidewalk; there was a special on Milk Duds and Snickers. Made him hungry. He hadn't eaten all day, thanks to a certain bear.

He crossed the street, cutting through the stand of pines in the town square. Dixie had to be around here somewhere. He wanted to be with her. Would so love to be taking her to see *Charade*. She intrigued him, wowed him, seduced him without even trying. One smile from Dixie and his whole life got a million times better. 'Course, once she found out who he really was he probably wouldn't have a life, because she'd beat him to a pulp for having lied to her. His only hope was to come clean as soon as possible and explain his actions. That he didn't take her into his confidence was not in his favor—more like an inscription on his tombstone.

He was having no luck finding her here, so he took off for the lake. The town wasn't that big so 5-K of anything had to involve the lake. The sun drenched the mountains in golds and purples that reflected in the water. Dixie stood by the abandoned boat rental, weather shutters closed, the place needing a coat of paint. She was gazing at the scene. No one else around. People in Whistlers Bend took the dinner hour seriously.

"We need to talk," he ventured as he approached.

She cut her eyes to him, a desperate glint there. "You want to talk? Here? Now? You and me? What a waste!" She threw her arms around his neck and kissed him. This was so much better than talking!

His heart slammed against his ribs, desire tore through him, frustration pushed him to the edge and he pinned her against the side of the building, taking her in his arms and nearly ravaging her on the spot.

His tongue captured hers, then hers did the same. Her breasts firmed against his chest and her legs parted; his erection nuzzled into her. She tugged his shirt from his waistband, her fingertips pressing into his skin.

"If we do this," she said… At least, that was what he thought she'd said, because he was sucking her lower lip into his mouth, distorting her speech right along with his brain. "We'll be on the front page of the *Whistle Stop*."

"No one's around. It's dinnertime." His tongue traced over her top lip.

"This is the Bend. Everyone knows everything. If this shop wasn't locked…"

He pulled out his wallet. Got a condom and held the foil package in his teeth as he took out a wire and wiggled it into the lock, springing it in record time. A man motivated. He snagged her hand, dragged her inside and kicked the door closed behind him. Rays of light slipped through the shutter slats. He unbuttoned his jeans as quickly as she undid her slacks. She yanked off her boots, then her jeans. He simply lowered his, not wanting to mess with boots again. He dropped his shirt onto the table, lifted her there, and as she wrapped her legs around his middle, he slid on the condom and then slid into her, his heart pounding, his desire for her stronger than any force on earth.

DIXIE FELT her head spin. How could she want Nick so badly when he was so…bad? He thrust into her again, then again, then he gripped her as his climax ignited hers. "Oh, Nick!"

"Dixie!" He hissed into the stillness. He kissed her neck, her ear, then claimed her mouth. He rested his cheek against hers. "Holy hell."

"I don't think it can be both."

"We just proved it can."

Meaning what? she wondered.

He framed her face between his palms and kissed her again.

"We just took friendship to a whole new level. What you do to me…" He exhaled. "What we do to each other. I—"

"Yoo-hoo. Anybody in there?" came Barney's voice from outside the bait shop.

"There's no one in there," said Ruth.

"I tell you I heard voices."

"That's just wishful thinking because you want the boat shop to reopen."

Nick's gaze met Dixie's and he made a *ssh* sound. He grabbed the door handle and held it in place as Barney tried to open it from the other side.

"See," said Ruth. "The place is locked up tighter than the Denver mint."

"I tell you I heard voices."

"It's your age. Give it up, old man, and I'll buy you a piece of apple pie at the Sage."

Nick stood still; Dixie didn't move, either, the sound of retreating footsteps on gravel fading. "That was damn close," he whispered into the stillness. "Being the brunt of town gossip is not my idea of fun."

But this was! Way too much fun. She studied Nick, wanting him again…right now! "We should leave separately. You sneak out first, then I'll follow. There's a path through the pines out back that leads into town."

His fingers raked through his mussed coal-black hair. "I hate sneaking around." He gazed at her for a moment. "Maybe we shouldn't sneak. Maybe we should get everything between us out in the open."

"The open?" Except he was a big fat lying smuggler. Okay, so he wasn't fat, but the lying smuggler was true enough. She didn't want to get that involved with him. But she was already involved majorly so. "We just made the jump from friend to…whatever. Maybe we should wait."

He smiled at her, a sincere warm smile, making her smile, too. "But I can't wait too long, Dixie girl." He turned, cracked the door and peered outside. "Remember to lock up and be careful out there." Then he slipped outside, his steps fading into the woods.

What a total mess, she thought as she shrugged into her jeans. She liked Nick a lot, tons in fact. And he was breaking the law big-time. But somehow, for some reason he didn't seem the type to do that.

Get a grip, Dix. What type was a smuggler? What did a smuggler look like? They didn't wear a bandana with the Jolly Roger emblazoned on it and a patch over one eye. But why would someone like Nick Romero, who seemed concerned about other people and their welfare, smuggle things that hurt so many? Nothing made sense.

She peeked outside to see if anyone was around, reset the lock and closed the door behind her. She headed into the trees, walked over pinecones and rocks till she got to the sidewalk. She looked both ways before easing out onto the town. She straightened her clothes and headed for the sheriff's office.

This whole situation had to end—she and Nick and the smuggling operation needed to be shut down before she went completely loopy. She'd turn this whole mess over to Jack and let him figure it out. No matter how attracted she was to Nick—and she was plenty attracted—she couldn't let him get away with smuggling.

She crossed the street and opened the sheriff's office door. BJ sat in a wood chair, holding a baby dressed in soft pink. Flynn stood behind her, looking happier than Dixie ever remembered him being, and Maggie and Jack gazing on.

"Well, isn't it just the gal we were looking for," BJ said. She beamed. "Come meet the newest adopted addition to the MacIntire family." She glanced up at Flynn. "And heaven knows there've been a lot of additions in the past month. We stopped in to introduce Angela to Jack, then Maggie came along, and now you're here. It's perfect." BJ smiled. "Everything's perfect."

Flynn kissed her. They trusted each other to the end of time. Dixie would give anything to have that trust with Nick. But once again her taste in men sucked. Dixie scooped the baby into her arms. "She's darling."

"We called Margaret and Drew and Petey in Martha's Vineyard. They're thrilled. I think they spent a whole day in New York shopping for the baby." She bit her lip. "I hope they can come home soon. The boys are really getting homesick."

Dixie handed Angela back to BJ. "That's why I'm here." She pulled in a big breath. "There's a break in the smuggling operation."

Jack folded his arms. "There is?"

Dixie continued before she could chicken out. "We should be able to put an end to this very soon. Fact is, someone in town connects to the smugglers."

Jack nodded. "We've decided that someone in town is a snitch. Whoever it is seems to be aware of when Roy and I are out or in town and makes a move then." His brows pulled together. "How'd you know?"

"Because I've been spending a whole of time with this snitch. Nick Romero's in with the smugglers."

Jack's jaw dropped a fraction. "Come again?"

Dixie held up her fingers to count the ways. "He has the merchandise in his house. I've seen it with my own eyes. He meets with trucks in the middle of the night. I've been there for that, too. He has the perfect cover and can break into locked buildings like no other." She blushed. "But the point is, these are not practices of a normal chef. The man's got more going on than his…cannelloni."

"Thought you liked my cannelloni," said Nick from the back hallway.

She spun around and blushed deeper. *Oh, damn!*

Not only had he caught her ratting him out, but he was clearly referencing their latest meeting at the bait shop. Guess turning in your lover *was* a bit over the top. But what else could she do?

He came into the room. Everyone's eyes went from her to Nick. Then everyone sat back and watched. The scene was like a blasted soap opera.

"So," he said as he stuffed his hands in his jean pockets, "you think I'm in with the smugglers."

She folded her arms, her gaze meeting his, neither backing down. "You are not just a chef."

"Have you looked at my place lately? If I'm not a chef, what's all that stuff doing there?"

"That doesn't mean there isn't more going on in your life than great recipes."

Jack picked up a paper from his desk and handed it to her. "I had Nick and Wes checked out. With the smuggling going on and strangers in town, it was a good idea." He nodded at the report. "He is just a chef, Dix. Wes is just a photojournalist. Period. This is from the Denver Police Department."

Dixie studied the paper, which listed places he'd worked, previous addresses. All very authentic. Feeling totally stupid and idiotic and completely mortified, she cut her eyes back to Nick. "Just a chef?"

His eyes softened. "Just a chef."

"I don't get it."

"Pots, pans, menus. Chef."

BJ stood. "Well, now that we've gotten that straightened out, I'm going to put Angela down." She studied Maggie, then Dixie. "Lend a hand? I'm new at the baby stuff. Just because I'm a doctor doesn't mean I can practice what I preach."

Okay, this was just a little embarrassing. But when Dixie Carmichael was wrong she was wrong, and not afraid to admit it. She faced Nick. "Then I owe you an apology. I'm sorry I accused you of smuggling."

He shrugged. "I'm nothing but an innocent by-stander with a spatula in my hand."

But he didn't seem like an innocent anything, and not just because he was dynamite in the sack. Something hummed below the surface besides spaghetti sauce. She knew it the way she knew when people ordered food at the Sage and wouldn't be able to pay for it, or if they were going to leave a big tip or were going to hit on her…she could just tell.

Dixie followed BJ and Maggie out to the street and helped BJ strap the baby in the stroller. "I'm not good company right now," she said. "I'm going to take off. I'll see you all tomorrow."

Without giving them time to protest, Dixie headed for Gracie's to get her car. Dusk hugged the town as the last rays of sunlight dropped behind the mountains. She wanted to be alone, think things out. Nick had completely upended her, in more ways than one.

Danny's Delight was available, and a perfect place to sort through this mess. To figure out how she could be so wrong about Nick Romero.

NICK GAZED ACROSS the sheriff's office from Flynn to Jack. "Oh, boy. When those three find out we've been lying to them about who I am, they are not going to take it well."

Flynn gave a dry chuckle. "They'll skin us alive because we didn't level with them right off."

"Who's leveling what?" Wes asked as he strode in through the back door.

"You wouldn't have to ask if you were here on time and not sniffing around Gracie Carmichael," Nick said.

Wes shrugged and there was a twinkle in his eyes. "Would I be doing that? This is business."

"Hell. Fooling-around business," Nick added. "But watch what you say near Gracie. If she and the other three realized what was going on, they'd be hounding us for information. Dixie would be glued to my hip to get her story, and BJ and Maggie wouldn't be far behind because they'd be watching out for Dixie."

"And because they're the nosiest females in Montana," Jack added. "We have to take our chances with the women finding out later rather than sooner. The three of them running around hunting for smugglers is not what we want right now."

He nodded to the back. "Being out here, where the whole town can see us together, is not a good idea. Let's go into the storage room. It's like a second office. For when we need to keep things quiet."

They trooped to the back and Jack turned to the map of the area, tacked on a big board. With a blue marker, he circled spots, saying, "I've been thinking about the smugglers meeting up. They're due to be here the night after next. There are five areas we should cover and five of us, counting Roy."

"We'll use satellite phones to keep in touch," Nick said. He peered at the others. "We'll be on our own out there and these guys are getting antsy. If we don't get them this go-round, I'm betting there won't be a next time. They'll move to another state and we'll have to start over searching for leads. None of us wants that. We get to nail these bastards so Dixie and Drew will be safe. No one takes these guys on their own. Call for backup. We all walk away from this in one piece."

His insides tightened as he gazed at the three men—great guys with a hell of a lot to live for. Jack was marrying Maggie, Flynn had a new family, Wes was getting real chummy with Gracie and he had… His restaurant? Hell of a substitute for Dixie. But once she wrote her story she was moving on, and that was that.

"Okay," Jack said, interrupting Nick's thoughts. "We

meet at Nick's night after next. We'll tell the women-folk we're having a poker night there. Mention cigars and there's no way they'll want to tag along or stop in."

Nick followed Wes out the back door of the office into the darkness, a single light brightening the stoop. "Heading to Gracie's?" he asked.

Wes gave him a half smile that seemed a little vulnerable and a lot happy. "She's a good woman, Nick. Her kids come first, she's true and caring and lots of fun, and she trusts me." The smile vanished. "Damn, I hate lying to her. Her no-good ex did that. Played her for a fool. He used her, double-crossed her, and now I'm doing the very same thing...sort of. Damn, I hate doing that."

Nick had never heard Wes talk this way. The bureau and whatever was needed to get the job done had always been his priority, until Gracie Carmichael dropped into his life. "Something about those Carmichael women."

Wes shook his head, determination etched on his face. "I don't want to leave Gracie, Nick. I've never met anyone like her, someone I connect with. But when she finds out I've lied to her and used her, she'll throw rocks at me."

"Tell Gracie you did all the wrong things for all the right reasons. For the national good. She'll understand and you could have a great time convincing her. She's not unreasonable and you didn't hurt her for personal gain. She understands that BJ will get her family back when this is all over and Dixie will be out of danger." He slapped Wes on the back. "It'll work."

"But I'm an agent. How will she feel about that? Things happen to agents and she doesn't need that danger for her children."

"From the sound of it I'd say you were headed to be an ex-agent, and when this is all over, there's no reason we can't pass you off as a concerned citizen, or a nosy photographer who got in the way. People might suspect otherwise, but they'll never be a hundred percent sure. You'll have to level with Gracie, of course, but you've already got a cover in place. Use that."

He fell into step beside Wes, who asked, "And what about you and Dixie?"

"In two days she'll have her story and be out of here, on her way to a life I want no part of." He nodded ahead. "Any special reason we're heading to Gracie's?"

"The wallboard's in and I'm going to help her paint, get the place ready for the grand opening."

Nick felt a grin split his face. "Paint? You? Have you ever painted anything?"

He blushed. "I painted her toenails the other night. Does that count?"

Nick chuckled. "I think it counts a hell of a lot."

The light was on in the Carmichael house, and

when Wes knocked, Katie and Cameron rushed for the door. They'd each drawn a picture for Wes, and said their mom was in the basement. Wes told them to lock the door and not answer without an adult present. Nick followed Wes down the stairs to the lower-level.

Gracie was bending over a paint can, stirring, but when she homed in on Wes, she had more than painting on her mind. Her lips turned into a warm welcoming smile.

"Hi, Nick," she said, her gaze glued to Wes. "If you're looking for Dixie, she's up at Danny's Delight. Needed time to hang out alone. Said for me not to, under any circumstances, tell you where she was." She cut her eyes to Nick for a split second and grinned. "Oops."

Anger mixed with fear lodged in Nick's gut. What was Dixie doing up in the mountains alone—*again?* Not saying anything to alarm Gracie, Nick gave her an appreciative smile and backed out the door, leaving the two lovebirds alone. He'd never seen Wes fall for anyone so fast. He'd never seen Wes fall, period. Go Wes! And Nick was heading out after Dixie, whether she wanted him there or not.

He shouldn't be doing that, of course. He should be hanging low till this job was over and he and Dixie would simply part… Except they were already involved whether he admitted it or not. He wanted to see her, be with her, make love to her. In a few days everything would change.

Streetlights blinked on as Nick made his way to his truck. The promise of fall licked the air. He paused for a moment on the sidewalk, looking at his restaurant, or what was supposed to be his restaurant. If it really were his, he'd paint the outside maroon and white and get a matching stripped awning. A sign saying Nick's Place in antique gold over the window; white concrete urns with red and white geraniums spilling over the top; a bistro table or two outside, where patrons could drink espresso or a glass of wine alfresco when the weather permitted; a fireplace inside for when the weather sucked.

But none of that was going to happen. Living in a town where everyone knew who he really was—or would soon know—wouldn't be a good idea. They could cover up Wes's identity, but the two of them together was too much. Nope, losing himself in another town was the best idea. Besides, Dixie, the biggest reason of all for staying in Whistlers Bend, was going for a big-time career.

He climbed in the truck, brought the engine to life and took off for Danny's Delight. He wound up the mountain, keeping a slow pace. He didn't need to go flying off the side again. Andy was still on the lam, could reappear at any time, and Nick sure didn't want to hurt Maggie's bull buffalo.

Nick smiled to himself. He fit in here, more easily than he'd ever imagined. He'd thought of himself
as a city boy, but now… Jack, Gracie, the Sage, the
surrounding mountains and lakes—he felt a part of
them all. As if he belonged, as if they'd chosen him
as one of them. That didn't happen often for Nick Romero. His mother had chosen alcohol and drugs; girl-
friends had chosen other mates, even Nonna Celest
had chosen to move to Italy. Not that he blamed her,
but she was gone all the same. And then there was
Dixie and her dreams of adventure that led her in the
opposite direction from his own plan to settle down.

Not much permanence in his life. Maybe that was
why he connected with the Bend. The town had been
here for over a hundred years; the mountains and
lakes, forever. The place oozed permanence, and he
liked that aspect more than he thought possible.

He passed lanes that led to weekend chalets. The
smugglers wouldn't chance a rendezvous at any of
those places in case owners or renters showed up un-
expectedly. No, the smugglers would meet in some
back road or a stand of trees like the one where he'd
seen them. They could hide for twenty minutes and
then be on their way.

He pulled onto the gravel that rambled its way to
Danny's chalet, following the creek as he'd done be-
fore. He found the driveway but didn't see Dixie's
Camaro. He killed the engine, the peace of night

welcoming him like a new friend. No truck motors rumbling along to indicate the smugglers had shown early. He examined the road he'd just driven over. His tracks and the narrow ones of the Camaro were visible, but no new ones, meaning Dixie was probably okay and had parked her car around back so he couldn't find her.

He walked up the path to the door. Only a portion of moon lit his way now. In two days, there'd be even less, making it the perfect time for smugglers to hook up. He, Wes, Jack, Roy and Flynn needed luck on their side. They'd be spread thin when they went smuggler hunting, with a lot of territory to cover.

There were no lights on inside the chalet. Was Dixie asleep? He doubted it. He knocked and yelled her name. When she didn't answer, he took out his handy-dandy lock pick and let himself in. Music came from the back of the chalet. "If I Could Turn Back Time." Cher? He remembered the photo that the guys at the bureau had slipped into his purse collection, the one that had helped Dixie reach the conclusion he was gay. Then he thought of Dixie, her great curls, tempting body, jazzy personality, and was reminded just how *ungay* he was.

He clicked on the rose-base lamp, illuminating the room. No Dixie sleeping on the couch...the couch where she'd helped with his boots and they'd made incredible love. "Dixie?"

When he got no answer, he headed down the back hall, past the bathroom that was bigger than his apartment bedroom. Lit candles flickered, the lingering scent of cedar and cinnamon permeated the air, bubbles billowed over a circular tub and Cher trilled a private concert. Wet footprints marked the cream-colored carpet that led on to the bedroom. He was following the prints when out of the corner of his eye he saw a flash of something that nearly missed his head.

"Nick?"

"Dixie?"

A wet, skimpy towel tied around her middle barely covered breasts to butt. She was gripping the dented saucepan from the last time they'd been here.

He grinned as he took in her big eyes, aggressive stance and delicious attire. "Do you always cook in the nude?"

She relaxed and gave him a sassy look. Damn, he liked that look. *He liked her way too much with any look.* He always felt alive when he was with Dixie Carmichael. Who wouldn't? "I am not nude. I have a towel and a weapon."

She held up the pot. "I thought you were a burglar, or one of those smugglers, and I had to protect myself. How'd you find me?" She scowled. "You don't have to answer that, because I already know the answer. A snitching sibling. No doubt to get rid of you so she could get Wes to herself. The woman's loopy over him."

"They are an item, aren't they." It was a statement, not a question, and Nick realized there was a hint of envy in his voice. Not that he didn't want Wes to be happy with Gracie, but he wanted Dixie to be happy with him, and that was not going to happen.

"You scared me to death."

"I called your name, but I guess your choice of music drowned me out."

She blushed and fidgeted. Not Dixie traits at all. She was uneasy about something and he suspected that something was him. Well, he was damn uneasy about her, too. Where did they go from here? Why the hell was he here in the first place?

"The song fit the occasion," she said. She let out a deep breath and folded her arms across her breasts, plumping them up over the top of the towel. "I really am sorry I ran to Jack and accused you of being a smuggler, but there was evidence and—"

"I found the bag, as I said, and wandered off exploring the hillside to find the best way to get my truck out. I heard trucks but didn't think much of it. The smugglers got there while I was away." Not to whip off that damn towel and feast his eyes on what was underneath took every ounce of control. But what did she have in mind? That was the big question.

She relaxed and a little smile played at her lips, which he'd really liked to kiss…while he ripped off the towel. She said, "I'm glad you're here."

"Really?"

"Absolutely." Her smile grew, and then she flipped the towel off her body.

Holy cow! She swung it around her head, doing a naked sashay—no one sashayed like Dixie Carmichael, naked or otherwise—laughing and giggling, before tossing it toward the bedroom. She threw her arms around his neck and kissed him hard. "I'm crazy about you, Nick, and I want everyone to see *us* together. We're more than friends and you're not a smuggler or gay and just a cook." She kissed him again. "You're a wonderful, fantastic cook. I couldn't be happier."

Oh, crap!

She Frenched him in the ear, sending chills down his spine and setting a fire in his belly.

"All these stupid feelings I had about you being something more than a chef were just a defense mechanism against me falling for you, I realize that now. The last thing I needed was to get involved with a man, any man, because I had these great plans, and then suddenly you showed up and I fell for you."

"You have…did…fall for me?"

She seemed startled. "And you haven't fallen for me?"

"Hell, yes."

She laughed. "Glad we got that straightened out." She kissed him again. "Come with me to Denver or Boston or wherever I go. Open your own restaurant. You'll be a success, and we can be together the way we are now and figure out our future."

He was dumbstruck. Dixie wanted to be with him? Wanted them to have a life together? She didn't want to leave him.

"Think about it." She slid his shirt up and coaxed it over his head, then swung it into the abyss to join her towel. She giggled as only Dixie could, and reached for his belt buckle. "I feel free, all my questions answered, all my worries about you over, and now I can enjoy being with you, Chef Nick Romero."

"I'm not perfect, Dixie."

"I don't need perfect. Perfect's boring. I need—" she looked him dead in the eyes "—to share my bubble bath with you. I want to make it up to you for treating you so shabbily and accusing you of terrible things you aren't guilty of." She pulled him by his belt toward the bathroom and kicked the door closed as Sonny and Cher sang "I Got You, Babe."

And how! He should resist. All her feelings for him were based on lies. But how the hell did a man resist a naked woman leading him by his belt buckle?

He had no flipping idea, especially when Dixie was doing the leading and he wanted more than anything to follow her.

She stopped by the tub that could pass for a small swimming pool and smiled up at him as she unzipped his jeans. He put his hands on her shoulders. "Dixie, are you sure about this? What if we aren't...compatible?"

She winked. "We proved we were beyond compatible the last time we were here."

"I don't mean just sex. This is more than sex. You want me to follow you to...wherever. Why?"

She laughed and slipped his jeans and briefs to his knees. "Because you're so well...*hung*. My, my, what have we here?"

His heart tightened. "You don't know me, Dixie."

She touched him, making his whole body hard. "Oh, I do. And getting more intimately acquainted every time we...meet."

"But—"

"And I appreciate that you love your grandmother, that you're compassionate and caring and forgiving and helpful and friendly and not afraid of bears."

"Terrified of bears."

She framed his face in her palms. "We get along, in and out of the tub, and if we let what we have go, we're nuts."

Maybe there *was* hope. Maybe somehow they could work their relationship out if, as soon as it was over, he came clean and made her understand what he was. "I need a day or two to figure things out."

She grinned. "But right now there's you and me and this wonderful tub." She placed both hands on his chest and gently pushed him till the backs of his legs connected with the tub. He sat on the edge and she tugged off one boot then the other. "I'm getting pretty good at this."

"I should quit wearing them. I'm thinking slippers."

Her lips nearly touched his, the sensation more provocative than actual kissing. She whispered against his mouth, "Want me to undress you or…"

"I'll do it." He could barely get the words out. "I'm faster." He stripped off his clothes and tossed his shirt in one corner, took a condom from his wallet and set it on the edge of the tub before tossing his jeans into another corner. She yelped as he lifted her into his arms. "Let's get slippery." And kissed her hard and settled them both into the bubbles.

"You don't look comfortable," she said, as he watched water slide off her lovely body. "And I really want you to be comfortable and relax."

"With that twinkle in your eyes and that devil smile on your lips, I doubt if there's one thing relaxing in what you have planned."

"Smart man." She kissed him, her silky body next

to his completely destroying any notion he had of discussing compatibility.

Being with her was heaven, and even if their relationship wasn't going to last, he didn't want her to hate him when this was all over. Somehow, someway, he'd explain everything to her and make her understand. He owed her that much.

But now… *Ah, hell,* now he was dying to just make love to her.

Chapter Nine

Nick let his body dissolve into the warm water, pushing aside the reasons he shouldn't be making love to Dixie, concentrating on all the reasons he should. He intended to enjoy her sparkling brown eyes taking him in; her laughter that made him laugh, too; her full shapely body gliding against his. "Damn, you're beautiful."

She captured a mound of suds in her hand, closed her eyes and blew them across the tub in a white frothy swirl. They danced in the candlelight and floated on the water. "I blew the suds before and made a wish." She faced him. "I wished for you, and now you're here. Who says wishes never come true."

He kissed her moist lips. "Oh, Dixie girl, not me."

"What do you wish for, Nick Romero?"

A clear conscience would be a nice start. "You any way I can have you."

She fixed a bath pillow behind his head as she

knelt beside him, the water lapping at her midriff, bubbles clinging to her breasts and the tips of her firm pink nipples. His finger traced the same path the suds took, left side, then right. He watched her breaths catch as he stroked her delicate skin, turning her on, making her aware how much he desired her. Her eyes clouded and she said, "You're cheating. I'm supposed to be tending to you, remember?"

"But I think we should play."

"My tub, my rules. Besides, I'm making it up to you for accusing you unjustly." She swiped his hands away.

"You can't expect me to sit here and do nothing."

"Oh, but I can." She smiled and kissed him and dropped a dollop of shampoo in her palm, then worked it into suds, her fingers slowly squeezing and rubbing, driving him into a frenzy just watching. Then she massaged his head, pressing gently into his scalp. "Close your eyes," she purred and lifted the water spray to rinse the suds away. He did as she'd asked, and then she kissed his eyes and nose as the suds slid down.

"My turn," he insisted as he opened his eyes.

"Not a chance." She pulled on a soft mitt and lathered it with something that hinted of flowers and seduction.

"I'll smell girly."

"You won't mind." She washed his chest, moving in slow, small circles over his tight pecs, then lower, to his waist.

"Oh, no, you don't," he said, knowing exactly where she was headed. He glided his arm around her to tug her under him. "This will be over before I get started."

She yelped and laughed as water splashed and suds piled up. His knees captured her hips; his arousal pressed into her silky abdomen. He placed the pillow to the back of her head and studied her radiant face. "Now it's my turn."

"You think that because you're bigger than me you can have your way?"

He kissed her, letting his tongue roam over her wet lips. "Yes."

Her breasts formed lovely mounds slightly above the water and were covered in bubbles. He gathered them up and set them aside. "I need to see you, all of you, as I make love to you." He watched her nipples tighten to hard pink nubs and her eyes dilate. She responded so completely to him, even his words, anticipating his lovemaking. She longed for him to touch her, exciting her even more, making love to her as only he knew how.

But not yet. "I intend to wash you."

Her legs snaked around his back, holding him secure. "I've got another idea." Her voice was strained. "I'm already clean."

He picked up the mitt. "It's my duty to be sure." He saw her hands reach for his erection but he intercepted them and held them together in front of her.

"What are you doing?"

"If you do what I think you're about to do, I'll never get my turn."

"This isn't fair."

He grinned, and using her words said, "You won't mind." Still holding her hands together, he kissed her slowly, letting his tongue take possession of every crevice of her delicious mouth. Then he stroked the sudsy mitt over her left shoulder, down to her wrist. "Nice hands. Nice everything."

She swallowed, passion pinking her cheeks and clouding her eyes. "Let me show you something else...nice."

He laughed, and massaged her other shoulder and arm. "I think you're clean here." He winked. "Now for the rest of you."

"Nick, this is so one-sided." She tried to free her hands again, but he kept them in place and rubbed the mitt across her sensitive nipples. Her eyes darkened as he tantalized her hard nubs. A whimper escaped her lips and he captured the delicate sound in his mouth.

She looked at him, her eyes smoky, her lips slightly parted. "I never knew making love could be like this."

"You're the perfect partner."

"Us together is perfect. I don't want this to end, Nick. I want you inside me every night."

And that was what he wanted, too, but he had no idea how to make it happen. He stroked under her breasts, down to her navel, then farther. Then he discarded the mitt and tangled his fingers in her soft curls. "You are so open for me, so ready."

"I was ready twenty minutes ago."

"Oh, but not like this." He released her hands and glided one finger into her heat, then two. Her sweet hot sex tightened and she gripped his shoulders and gasped. "Nick? I can't…"

Her body shuddered in the first throes of climax. He used the condom, then replaced his fingers with himself. Bracing against the edge of the tub, he started the long steady rhythm that drove every thought about smugglers and lies and the FBI from his brain, and reveled in making love to this incredible woman.

She arched her hips, meeting his thrusts each time, till she yelled his name once, then again, as they climaxed.

He swished her on top of him as they relaxed in the warm water, Dixie's breathing slowing, as did his. The rise and fall of her breasts against his chest was reassuring and he knew that what bound Dixie and him was beyond sex. Every inch of him hungered for this being together to last forever, just as she'd said. But how to make it happen? "I need to clean up," he finally managed to say.

He climbed from the tub, dripping water as he got rid of his condom and grabbed a towel. When he turned back to the tub, Dixie was out, still naked, thank heavens—waiting for him with a towel of her own and wicked glint. "I want to dry you off."

"Me, too." He patted her face as she did likewise, then her chest and his and beyond. Each stroke, pat and rub he received, and the ones he gave, turned him on again. How could the strong desire he had for Dixie happen so fast? But now wasn't the time for questions. He dropped the towel, swept Dixie into his arms and headed for the bedroom as she wrapped hers around him and made him feel that there was no one else on the planet but the two of them in a chalet in the mountains.

DIXIE AWOKE the next morning to the smell of fresh coffee, as sunlight streamed through the chalet's floor-to-ceiling windows. Nick was gone, but he'd left a note on the pillow next to her. She sat up and read—"Went for grub. Be back soon. Don't get out of bed. Think horny thoughts."

She smiled and flopped back with a big dopey grin on her face. Guess "gone for grub" meant he couldn't settle for a breakfast of Pop-Tarts and orange juice, though he'd obviously drunk the coffee. It smelled much better than anything she'd ever made. Hers was either too strong and tasted like paint thinner, or too weak.

Gravel crunched in the driveway and a car motor died. She tossed off the covers to go meet Nick. If she met him nude, the way she was now, who could predict where that would lead. Just in case he wasn't sure... She grabbed her lipstick from her purse and drew circles around her breasts and an arrow down her middle, pointing to her most strategic spot. Then she plucked a dried rose from the arrangement next to the bed, clamped the flower between her teeth and pranced into the living room—as Danny entered the chalet, followed by an obviously pregnant Charity, who was yelling, "Work, work, work. All you do is go to the office and—"

Her tirade stopped as all eyes focused on Dixie's lipstick artwork. Dixie spat out the rose and grabbed two pillows from the couch to cover exposed places, though her arrow was too long to cover completely.

"Dixie!" Danny said.

She smiled. "Uh, hi?" She swallowed. "Nice seeing you both again. Charity, you seem well. I didn't realize you'd be here today. Either of you. But obviously, *I* am." Gads, she was rambling like an idiot. And with two pillows clamped to her body, she looked like one.

Danny ran his hand through his thinning sandy hair. "Hell, I didn't know I was going to be here, either." He glanced at Charity. "And I wouldn't be if my wife hadn't dragged me." He glared at Dixie. "And what the hell's going on with that red arrow?"

Dixie forced a grin. "Directions?"

Charity put her hands on her hips. "It's either *we* talk here, or we have our attorneys do the talking. I'm fed up, Danny. You hear me? Completely fed up."

Dixie backed into the bedroom as Danny said to Charity, "Dammit all, I have to make the money. Who do you think pays for those spa treatments you run off to, or those trips to New York and Rome for clothes?"

Just like old times, except she wasn't the one after Danny to stop working himself into a grave and she'd never gone to the spas and or bought her clothes anywhere other than the mall in Billings.

She slipped into her robe, and contemplated sneaking out the back, except she really wanted a Pop-Tart and some of that coffee. She returned to the living room as Charity was shouting, "Well, I'm not raising this baby alone."

Dixie felt like one of those referees in a boxing ring. She needed a whistle to bring round one to an end. "Coffee anyone? Or juice? Maybe water?" *Prozac!*

"If it's got a Jack Daniel's chaser, you can count me in," Danny said.

Dixie smiled sweetly, because not being married to Danny suddenly felt really, really good. It hadn't always felt that way, of course. When he'd announced he wanted to get rid of her, she'd cried and thrown things and felt like a loser, but now… She was beyond him. Beyond babies and a house in the burbs and a husband who thought the world revolved around him and couldn't get that it didn't. She was forty and had a life of her own, and it was pretty darn good.

But that was her. This was Danny and Charity, who had a baby on the way. Maybe she could help. She owed Danny for divorcing her. She headed for the kitchen and called over her shoulder, "You both must be exhausted after your trip."

"Hell, I sure am. And exhausted from this constant nagging." Danny followed Dixie, then Charity did the same. They sat across from each other at the maple table, staring daggers as Dixie served up orange juice and coffee.

Danny drank his coffee and glanced at Dixie. "Hey, this is damn good. You finally learned to cook?"

Ah, yes, Danny the charmer. Why hadn't she thrown a party when he'd left? Hey, there was still time. She said to Charity, "You want a daddy for your baby and you don't want to be carting Danny off for triple bypass." She pointed to Danny. "Don't you get it? She wants you around, buster, and I'm here to tell you not everyone does."

"That wasn't very nice." Danny pouted.

"Sorry. It kind of slipped out. But it's the truth.

Think about what you're doing, Danny. Don't mess up your life for a few extra dollars." Dixie watched as Charity's eyes softened. She loved Danny and he probably loved her or he wouldn't have driven all the way to the chalet to try to work things out. Danny didn't do anything that he really didn't want to.

The front door opened. "Hey, Dixie girl," came Nick's voice. His footsteps sounded on the hardwood floor as he approached. "Whose Lexus is—" He stopped in the entrance to the kitchen, grocery bag in hand, gazing from Danny to Charity and held up the dry rose to Dixie.

She slid the rose behind her ear and slipped her arm through his. "Nick Romero, this is Danny Juriack, my ex, and his lovely wife, Charity."

"So you're the one she's drawing directions for," Danny huffed.

Dixie reddened and Nick eyed her questioningly, but before he could ask, she asked him, "Think you have enough in that bag for four superb omelets?"

He grinned. "You bet." He glanced at Danny, then back to Dixie. "If that's what you want."

Words she'd never heard from her ex in all their years of marriage. She grinned in return and held Nick a bit tighter. "Thank you. I appreciate it."

And she really did. She owed Danny a good breakfast for showing up and reminding her just how lucky she was to have Nick Romero in her life and

not him. And she realized she truly did want him to
be happy.

DIXIE FLOATED THROUGH the dinner rush hour at the
Sage like those bubbles in the tub she'd shared with
Nick. Ah, Nick! She filled coffee cups and served up
daily specials, special orders and everything in between. Evan Bucky Daniel's temper tantrum in the
middle of the diner didn't faze her. She simply
stepped around him…though you'd think a fifty-
year-old man wouldn't get so upset over the Sage
running out of peanut butter pie.

The dinner crowd thinned as the coffee and dessert patrons meandered in, including Maggie. She
parked at their usual table and waved at Dixie as if
flagging down a New York taxi. Looking haggard,
BJ slid into the next chair and held up a cup, des-
perately signaling that the cup was empty. Dixie
snagged a carafe of hot water and a pack of herbal
tea and made her way to the table. Her dinner shift
was over now and she was more than happy to give
the job to the night-shift girls. She took in Dixie and
BJ. "You two are *so* demanding. And you never leave
big tips."

"But we buy you great Christmas presents." BJ
tore open the covering for the teabag with her teeth
and frantically dunked the gauzy package into the hot
water. "I have to find an assistant."

Dixie parked her hand on her hip. "Honey, I got news. Nobody can have that baby but you."

BJ growled and gave her a beady-eyed look. "Funny, very funny. I mean an assistant doctor, or a medical assistant. Right now, I'd settle for a witch-doctor with a bone through his nose. When the boys come back from their vacation, and I have three to deal with, and one on the way, I'm toast."

Maggie sipped her coffee as Dixie sat down. "Where's Angela now?"

"Flynn's taking her for a walk. The menfolk are getting together a big poker game for tomorrow. Cigars were mentioned. Gross. How can a doctor's husband smoke?"

Maggie laughed. "If you think you can control Colonel Flynn MacIntire just because you married him and you're a doctor, you are so wrong."

BJ suddenly laughed, too. "But it's so much fun to try. Besides, sometimes I win. And sometimes he wins." She giggled. "I really like when he wins and he tries to make it up to me, or I make it up to him."

"The honeymoon's not over," Maggie said on a laugh, then added, "since the men are having a night out, we should do the same."

BJ sighed. "I'll have Angela. I don't want to get a sitter so soon."

Maggie clasped her hand. "Of course you have Angela. We'll all help care for her, and what I have in mind is very Angela-friendly. I'll make my secret 'Death by Chocolate' cake and we'll feast."

"And you'll want us to hunt through magazines and critique wedding dresses," Dixie added.

"That is because you still haven't found something I like, even after you promised. Come on," she whined. "I'm desperate. I have two days to order a dress before it's too late." She studied Dixie. "What's up? You have a weird expression on your face."

"This is my chance to get the smugglers."

"Can't you just forget them for one night?" Maggie huffed. "Think food, think chocolate."

Ignoring her, Dixie pushed on. "This is perfect. You two can cover for me in case Nick calls. There's little moon tomorrow night. The time's perfect for the bad guys to meet up again. I bet they hook up once a week or less to offload goods. That's how long it would be for them to get to cities and sell to vendors, then head back for the next shipment. Boy, I bet they're making a killing. And this is just one part of the operation."

"Dixie," BJ hissed. "You're going to get yourself killed."

"It's not like that," Dixie countered. "I'm going to report. If I find something, I'll call it in to Jack. I'm not the marines."

BJ drummed her fingers on the table. "Nick will never ever approve of you going out alone."

Dixie drew herself up tall—as tall as five feet three inches got sitting down. "I do not need him or any other man to bless what I do. I sure don't bless his cigar smoking. Besides, nothing's going to happen. I'm going to sneak and snoop and poke around and get enough information to get a story, maybe get a few pictures."

"Maybe get your head blown off."

She begged. "Come on, help me out here. Just make like I'm with you for a few hours in case Nick calls, which I don't think he will because of the poker thing."

BJ took another sip of tea. "All right, all right. But only because I know what it's like to have a dream you want so bad you can taste it. But no confronting smugglers. Promise?"

"We'll meet at Sky Notch at eight," Maggie said. She peered at Dixie. "Maybe I should go with you. Maybe Andy's out there waiting for me."

"I'll keep an eye open. The two of us yelling 'Here buffalo, buffalo, buffalo' is not conducive to snooping around bad guys." She nodded to Nick, Jack and Flynn, who were walking through the door. "Remember, girls night out, nothing more."

"Hey," Jack said as the three men and Angela in the stroller, drew up to the table. "What's going on? You three got something cooking? You're awfully quiet all of a sudden."

Darn, Dixie thought. *How'd he know?* "Blueberry pie," she said, at the same time that Maggie said, "Wedding dresses," and BJ said, "Babies."

Dixie laughed. "See? Lots going on." She pointed at the next table. "If you men would shove these together, we'll have enough room for everyone."

"You know," BJ offered as she snatched up Angela, "since there're six of us, maybe it's time to find a new table." She pointed across the diner to a booth with chairs at the ends. "Like that one. Seats six, no problem. Even room for a high chair."

"Or two," Dixie said, trying to sound enthusiastic but not feeling that way at all. Not just because they were leaving their table of thirteen years, but because soon five people would be sitting there, not six. Dixie Carmichael was leaving the Bend. Well, this was her decision, her dream to follow, and she wasn't going to get morose about it or let anyone else feel that way.

She slapped her palm on the tabletop, getting everyone's attention in the diner. "Follow me," she said as she hitched her chin toward their new digs. "Time for us to make a change."

The three women stood and gazed at their old table, then across to the new booth. BJ bit at her bottom lip; Maggie touched the tabletop. "All I care is, thank goodness this table can't talk. It could blackmail us for all we're worth."

Everyone in the diner laughed, Dixie handed each a knife, fork and spoon, and the six of them, with Angela in her stroller, paraded across the diner to the new table.

After christening the spot by eating lemon meringue pie, they all walked home, Nick falling into step beside Dixie. Crickets chirped the last choruses of summer as warmth gave way to a chill off the mountains. She snuggled close to Nick, to keep warm and simply because she liked the feel of him at her side. "Wes is helping Gracie paint again tonight," she said. "Never seen so little get done in so many hours."

"Why don't you spend the night with me. Then you won't have to worry about interrupting anything."

"But I don't have my pjs."

He draped his arm around her, making her warm all over. "I won't tell if you won't. Besides, I have something waiting for you at my place."

"The way it's been going between us, you've always got something waiting for me, and we sure as heck don't need to be at your place to…use it. Not that I'm complaining."

"I bought you a present, sort of."

"For me?" They paused under the streetlight and he turned her collar up against the breeze. She said, "I want a hint. Just a little one. What's the first letter? The last? What color?"

"Nosy is your middle name." He kissed her. "You'll have to wait till we get home." His eyes met hers and the last word hung between them. *Home*. They were going there together now, but how many more nights would they be together like this, teasing and joking and having a great time? As soon as she scooped her story, she was gone, right? That was what she wanted most, right?

"One teeny hint?"

He nodded down the street to his place. "Not a chance, but we can run the rest of the way and you'll find out faster than if we walk."

"You're on." She grabbed his hand and took off running as she had when she was a teenager, feeling happy and alive with someone special in her life. And Nick Romero was that and more.

Panting, she reached the front door. "You're not even out of breath and I'm ready to die on the spot. You're in pretty good shape for a chef."

"All those hours cooking are great exercise." He found his key and unlocked the door. Inside, he clicked on the light. The new fixtures he couldn't resist installing bathed the room in a soft glow. "How do you like the stucco finish and terrazzo floor?"

"Terrific, wonderful. Now, cough up my prize before I get crabby. I didn't run all this way for my health...though I probably should start."

He folded his arms and stared down at her. "I need some incentive."

"Like?"

"Like this." He swept her into his arms and kissed her long and thoroughly. "Damn," he said. "I've been wanting to do that since I walked into the diner."

She laughed as he set her back on her feet. "Well, why didn't you just do it? No one would have minded, certainly not me."

He nodded at two FedEx boxes on the floor. "There's your present."

"Guess this rules out a Porsche or tennis bracelet."

He got a knife from the kitchen and handed it to her. "Your present. You get to do the honors."

She hunkered down and he joined her as she sliced through the packing tape. She put down the knife, drew back the flaps and peered in. "Blue T-shirts?"

"With pink lettering." He snapped one from the box and held it up for her to see. "Whistlers Bend now has its first official 5-K Run T-shirt."

"*Whistle For The Cure*. Oh, my gosh, I love it."

"There are pink whistles in the other box. Thought it would be fun."

"It's…fabulous. Ingenious. Thank you." She flung her arms around him, knocking him to the floor, her on top, as she kissed him forehead-to-chin and everywhere in between, making them both laugh.

"I think I'll get some area rugs for this floor—it's

damn hard. And if I'd known the T-shirts would get this response from you, I'd have gotten them a lot sooner."

She ran her hand over his stubbled chin and tweaked his nose. "This is the best present anyone's ever given me. I mean that—I really do."

He sobered and wrapped his arms around her back. "Why does this mean so much to you? You never said."

"I had a lump and it scared the crap out of me. Mine was benign, but it sure made me think of all the women who didn't get such great news. Over a million women will be diagnosed with breast cancer this year. Over forty thousand will die in the U.S. alone."

"And you wanted to do something."

"Obviously, so did you." She stared at him, appreciating him for the wonderful compassionate man he was. No rough-and-tumble alpha male here, charging around. Just…Nick, the guy who got the job done and cooked like no other.

"Where do we go from here, Dix?" he asked in a quiet voice. "Because I don't know how to make whatever is going on between us work. I can't ask you to stay here. Working at the *Whistle Stop* isn't the big newspaper job you always wanted. Even if you broadened the base and united the other newspapers in the surrounding areas so the news included more towns, it would still be a very small-town newspaper."

"Guess this means you're not following me to who-knows-where."

"I hate who-knows-where."

"I'll be back and visit. You can make me ziti and I'll love it."

He smiled, but the smile didn't reach his eyes. "Sure. It's a deal. But now we have tonight, all night, unless you're hell-bent on disrupting your sister and Wes."

"She'd so wring my neck. You're stuck with me, Nick Romero."

"I want longer, Dixie girl. A lot longer. But until I figure out how to make that happen, I'll settle for us together one night at a time."

Chapter Ten

Nick stood in the middle of his kitchen and listened to a radio station in Billings that broadcast sports talk shows. With all the voices and chatter coming from this channel, it would sound like a poker game going on tonight even if there wasn't one.

He puffed on a cigar, trying to enjoy the experience, then studied the glowing tip and frowned. No, nothing had changed from the last time he'd given cigars a whirl while on that job in Miami. He still hated cigars. The back door opened and he puffed the cigar again. If it was Dixie, he didn't want her hanging around. The smoke and odor would drive her out in record time. He almost left himself. He plastered a smile of enjoyment on his face as his stomach rolled.

"What the hell are you doing?" Wes asked as he came in the door.

Nick dropped the smile. "Getting real sick." He

took another drag. "I can't do this. You're my partner. It's your job to stink up the place."

Wes frowned. "You're a little green there, buddy."

Nick waved the cigar over the kitchen table, strewn with cards, empty beer bottles, chips and half-eaten dip and sandwiches. "Dixie is the soul of nosy. Her dropping by because she or BJ or Maggie can't get one of us on our cells is a big possibility. This place has to look like we've been here and maybe stepped out, or she'll get suspicious and go snooping the way she always does. It's just a matter of time before she connects me to the smugglers and puts me on the law-enforcement side of this job, since I didn't fit on the smuggling side. If that happens, she'll never let me out of her sight, thinking I can lead her to her story."

He took one more drag and snuffed out the gross-tasting stogie. "When I have my restaurant, there will be no smoking of any kind anywhere."

"And where is that going to be? Seems to me the Bend is a regular haven for the ex-macho types. Jack's doing okay and you know he made his share of enemies in Chicago. Flynn's been watching soldiers' backs for almost twenty years and is ready to retire, and I'll be here. I figured we could kind of look out for one another. Maybe you should consider staying."

"Three Musketeers style."

"It can be four…or more."

Nick studied him. "That means you've decided to stay?"

"I'm going to get Gracie to take me if I have to wait till doomsday and woo her with every flower and box of chocolates west of the Mississippi. Her kids are great. Never been around kids much. I regret that. Maybe this is my second chance. I'm sure going to try."

Footsteps sounded in the front room. Jack, Flynn and another guy about their age crowded into the kitchen. Jack nodded at the table. "Good cover, but we won't need it. The women are hanging out at Maggie's tonight, eating chocolate cake, saving none for us, and planning our wedding."

Flynn slapped him on the back. "Think elopement."

"Did that the first time and Maggie's not going to let me get away with it again. She's inviting the whole damn town. I got her talked out of me wearing a freaking tux. That's the best break I got."

A soft grin parted his face. "But she sure is worth all this hassle. And before I get too sappy—" he nodded at the man beside him with the week's growth of beard, flannel shirt, beat-up cowboy hat, leather vest and piercing blue eyes "—this is Sam Maxwell, Whistlers Bend's answer to Indiana Jones and then some. He owns and operates Adventures Unlimited, that big log cabin Flynn's brothers are building up in the mountains."

Sam nodded and Jack continued. "Roy's picked

up some kind of flu bug, and Sam here's going to take his place. He knows these mountains the way he knows his name."

Sam shook hands with Wes and Nick. A grip like that suggested Sam Maxwell didn't push a pencil for a living; that was for damn sure. "Thanks for helping out," Nick said.

"Don't need smugglers giving the Bend and the mountains a bad name," Sam said. "My customers come to hike, fish, kayak, canoe, camp out and get away from city crime, and here it is on my doorstep." He rubbed his hand over his beard. "I just got back with a group doing two weeks of canoeing and hiking. That's why I look like hell."

Jack spread the map over the cards and poker chips. He pointed to the circles he'd drawn two days earlier. "Nick, you cover the area between the old depot and the south road. That's where Danny's Delight is. You've been over that area before. Wes, you take the roads off the expressways. That way you won't get lost in the mountains and can keep us posted if you see the trucks heading our way. Sam covers the places around his cabin, down to the expressways, and Flynn and I will take the middle sections."

Nick opened a backpack and pulled out six cell phones an agent from Billings had dropped off earlier. "These are satellite. Our numbers are taped to the back. No one takes these guys alone. There were five the one time I crossed their path, and it's a good bet they're armed. We all meet up, surround them and surprise the hell out of them. They don't have a chance to get to their weapons. Any questions?"

Flynn shrugged and gave a crooked smile. "No jackets with FBI across the back? No army of a hundred? That's the usual FBI way, right?"

Wes laughed. "Bells and whistles, except tonight. We're keeping this low-profile so as not to tip off the source of the smuggling. We get these guys and cut a deal where they rat out their contacts, and we go nail them. We keep it up till we snag the big dogs."

"Here's another question," Jack groused as he crunched a pretzel he'd snagged from an open bag on the table. "When do I get more of this Italian food? I'm starved. Maggie spent all day baking that chocolate cake. I licked the damn spoon and did the dishes."

Nick chuckled. "I'll cook for your wedding. How's that?"

Jack nodded. "You're on." He handed Nick and Wes maps, and they all took their phones. "We'll leave one at a time," Jack added. "So it doesn't look like a damn Easter parade marching out of here. Even if it's night, someone around here's always watching."

Jack left, then Wes, followed by Sam and Flynn. Out of habit, Nick checked his pocket for his SIG 226 as he closed the restaurant door behind him. His shotgun was already in the truck under the seat; another gun was laced to his ankle. He hadn't carried a weapon all the while in the Bend and he'd felt kind of naked. Then he thought about when he really was naked and who he was naked with. Dixie—all warm and soft and making love sounds—sure beat the hell out of the night ahead of him. Later, maybe he'd catch up with her.

Dixie was something else, had her nose into everything, and he was damn glad she was eating chocolate cake with Maggie, BJ and the baby. 'Course, there'd be hell to pay when she found out he hadn't played poker and had gone after the smugglers without her, but that was just one more deception to add to a really, really long list.

Maggie cut another piece of cake for Dixie as BJ said, "Thought you were going on a diet."

"I'm trying. I had cereal for breakfast. I've got a working night ahead of me. Got to keep up my strength. And I'm drinking a diet cola." She held it up to prove her point. "What more do you want from me?"

"How about twenty pounds?" BJ countered.

"I think Jack bought our little woman's night out," Maggie said. She sat down beside BJ. "He's not going to be happy when he finds out the truth." She turned to Dixie. "Nick will probably bust a gut when he hears about you going off into the mountains alone."

"This is not a problem," Dixie said as she swiped crumbs from her mouth and congratulated herself on not cutting a third piece of cake. "You didn't lie. None of us did. This is a woman's night out, and we are eating the cake like we said. I'm simply leaving a little early and going home by way of some mountain roads."

"If you think Nick's going to fall for that line of bull," Maggie said, "you live in a dream world. He may be the mild-mannered man about town, but I'm sure even he gets upset sometimes, and I bet this is going to be one of those times. If you happen to see Andy, though, let me know. My hands and I are going out tomorrow to round him up. I've bought every Peep in three towns to get the job done. I've got to get him if Dan Pruitt and I are going to increase our number of beefalo. That boy's going to work overtime to service all those females waiting impatiently for him."

BJ fed Angela the last of her bottle. "Sounds like every male's dream job."

Dixie laughed and said, "Speaking of males and their dreams…I wonder if Danny and Charity are still at the chalet."

Maggie glanced her way, eyes wide. "I didn't know they were at the chalet. Weren't you and Nick there? Gee, that must have been cozy."

"Actually, it was…revealing. Danny's a jerk, and I really get that now, and Nick isn't, and I get that, too. He cooked breakfast for us."

"The man's a saint," BJ said. "I loved that article you did on him panning for gold and the bear sneaking up on him. The pictures were priceless. Everyone in town laughed and so did Nick. No big ego in the way. The man's comfortable with who he is."

"What are you going to do about Mr. Romero?" Maggie added. "Up and leave the best guy who ever entered your life?"

"You're saying that because you don't want me to go."

"There is that. But it is true."

Dixie pushed the cake around her plate, suddenly not hungry. "So, what about my dream job?"

"What about your dream *man*?" BJ offered. "He's the prefect complement to you. You're a loose cannon and he's a homebody. Cooks, putters with rehabbing, buys his grandmother nice gifts, and not an aggressive bone in his entire gorgeous, generous body. He's just what you need. Sedate, responsible, honest, trustworthy, dependable."

"Sounds like a Boy Scout," Dixie huffed.

"Bet you don't think *boy* after the lights go out," Maggie said.

"All right, all right." Dixie threw up her hands. "I get the point. I love you all, too."

"But do you love Nick?" BJ asked. "That is the real question here, isn't it?"

Did she? If she loved him, really loved him, she wouldn't leave him and run off. Then again, if he loved her, wouldn't he follow her? Except, he hated the big city, for whatever reason. She didn't hate Whistlers Bend; she just wanted to follow her heart. Was Nick her heart?

Maggie checked her watch. "You better go if you want to get back by midnight."

Dixie pulled on a black fleece and added a black baseball cap, putting it on backward and tucking her hair underneath. She did a slow turn to show the cap off. "My official snoopy reporter attire."

"Suits you," Maggie said. "Keeps those moonbeams off your neck…if there are any out there." She handed her a plastic Baggie. "Peeps. If you find Andy, give him a treat." She hugged Dixie. "Two hours and you're back, okay? Anything longer and I'm calling Jack myself and turning you in. You're not going to confront the smugglers—just find clues, right?"

Dixie left, got into the Camaro and headed for the back roads, bouncing over ruts till her headlights picked out the old depot. The weathered door swung lazily in the night breeze; the roof drooped a bit more in the front. "I wonder if this old place can withstand another winter," she said to herself. She'd grown up with that depot; it had been here all her life. And now she wasn't going to be here.

She pulled around to the rear, killed the engine and decided to walk. She wouldn't cover as much territory, but a car was a dead giveaway. She swiped her flashlight around the area. Nothing. She'd head down toward Danny's chalet, keeping off to the side, in the trees. That was where Nick had found the Tiffany bag. Maybe the smugglers would stop there again, or maybe they'd left something else behind.

She tripped twice and stubbed a toe once, but a dozen devoured marshmallows and an hour and a half later, she had zilch to show for her pain. What a completely wasted night. She retraced her steps to the depot, cutting through the trees to the back to save time. She climbed into the Camaro, pulled out her keys, checked her rearview mirror—and saw a strange man with a gun staring back at her. "Didn't your mama teach you to lock your car?"

"Didn't yours teach you not to sneak up on people?"

Oh, crap. Dixie felt her heart hit her stomach. She'd wanted to find the smugglers, but she'd had no intention of them finding her. Surprise, surprise!

"Do what I say and I'll let you go."

Phew. At least she was safe…sort of.

"Get out of the car and go around to the front so I can keep an eye on you while we finish up business. What the hell are you doing up here at this time of night, anyway? We saw your car and wondered where you were."

Looking for you! She sure couldn't say that. Instead, she went with, "Looking for a buffalo."

She got out of the car and added, "I own a ranch nearby and am raising a new kind of herd, one sired by a buffalo." She studied the man out of the corner of her eye as they walked in the path of his flashlight. Big flannel shirt, scruffy. Did he buy her story?

"You really expect me to believe you're here for a buffalo?"

"They're…nocturnal. And he escaped into the mountains. Do you know how much a buffalo costs? Lots." She pulled a marshmallow from her pocket. "They love these things. I'll hold the flashlight. Try some. Pretty good, especially the purple ones. Since you're not going to shoot me, I'm willing to share."

He took the purple bunny and she held a flashlight as they walked around the side of the depot to the front. "They'd be better stale," he said.

"That's what everyone says."

Headlights from a small truck illuminated the depot and a younger man joined them. The guy with the gun said to her, "Sit down and don't move. In twenty minutes this is all over with and you can walk home."

"I have a car."

"Not going to be much good to you once I shoot out the tires."

She tsked. "Do you have to? They cost a hundred bucks a piece."

The younger man glared at her. "You'd rather we shoot something else?"

"Good point." What a grouch. No Peeps for him. She offered the older man another one. "All I have left is pink."

Chewing marshmallows and keeping an eye on her, the man headed toward the truck by the trees and opened the back doors. What sounded like a larger truck approached, headlights cutting the dark. A large paneled truck followed. Three men got out and all came over to the depot. They stood gazing down at her.

Dixie opened the bag. "Peep anyone?"

"What the hell's this?" a man in a red parka asked. "Martha Stewart's welcoming committee?"

The guy with the gun said, "She was up here trying to capture a buffalo when we showed up."

"A what?" the red-parka man growled. "Are you hitting the sauce again, Tom?"

"A buffalo. That's what she said, I swear. Did you know buffalo are nocturnal?"

"He's telling the truth," Dixie added. Though she made up the nocturnal part. "There really is a buffalo. Andy. And I was out searching for him."

Parka man shook his head. "We've met you—you're that nosy waitress from the Purple Sage. Always asking questions and poking around. And now you're after us. I don't buy that buffalo story for a minute."

He gave her a wicked laugh that made her skin crawl. "Well, chickie, you went and found us. Now what are you going to do about it?"

"And you're one of the guys who came after Drew." She stood and put her hands to her hips, her anger overriding her fear. "How could you scare a little boy like that?"

"Lady, you are one nosy broad. This time a little too nosy for your own good. Sit down and shut up."

NICK FELT EVERY CELL of his body sizzle as he aimed his binoculars through the trees to Dixie. She stood in the middle of five smugglers, silhouetted in their headlights…feeding them marshmallows? He shook his head to clear his vision, because this really couldn't be happening, could it? Hell, yes! When it came to Dixie Carmichael, anything was possible.

He could see his report now: *The hostage was feeding her captors Peeps.*

He hunkered down behind a rock and pressed in Jack's number, then gave him a quick rundown of the situation. Jack's graphic response nearly melted the phone and probably sent the satellite into another orbit. He told Nick to sit tight, that he and the rest of the guys would be there in seven minutes flat.

But there was no way Nick was staying put with Dixie in harm's way. He sure couldn't go in with guns drawn, but he was going in. He wasn't about to let her face those guys alone except for a bag of marshmallows.

He got up and ambled toward the group with his hands raised. "Hey, Dixie, is that you?" he called. "What are you doing up here in the middle of the night?"

Immediately, one of the men came toward him, gun drawn. "Stop right there," he yelled. "What the hell is this—a damn convention?"

Nick asked in his most innocent voice, "What's going on, guys? Are you lost?"

"Nick?" Dixie said. "You're supposed to be playing cards at your restaurant."

"Had a run of bad luck. Thought I'd take a walk, instead."

"All the way up here?"

"Hitched a ride with Dan Pruitt, who was on his way home from the Cut Loose."

The parka man said to Nick, "Get over there with that woman. Your luck's just got a whole lot worse."

Two more men approached, one sporting a baseball cap and another gun. Dixie said, "I'm the one you want here. I'm the one who's the reporter and been trying to find you guys so I could scoop a story.

Let Nick go. He's just a cook, opening a new restaurant in town and not anybody you need."

"Oh, really." It was a statement, not a question. The man in the parka started to laugh and Nick felt alarm bells go off in his head. This guy knew something about him and it was more than Nick the cook.

Dixie nodded. "Yeah, really. The only thing he's after is Emeril's recipe for calamari, and the right wine to go with it. How about this? I'll stay with you and you let him go. Even if Nick can recognize you, it doesn't matter all that much. You guys are like smoke, floating around here and there. No one can catch you. They have no idea where to look."

"You did," the baseball guy quipped.

"Technically, you caught me, so it doesn't count. Let Nick start walking back to Whistlers Bend. By the time he reaches anywhere that resembles civilization, you all will be long gone out of here."

The man in the parka gazed at Nick and said, "She really does think you're a cook. That is so rich. I bet you fed her a string of lies that would choke a horse."

He nodded to Dixie. "Sweetheart, I hate to be the one to tell you this, but your nice sweetie-pie man here is a big, badass FBI agent."

This time Dixie laughed. "No, no, no. You got the wrong guy. Nick's just a cook—well, not *just* because his ziti is to die for. For a while I thought he was gay, and then I thought he was a smuggler, but…"

Parka man's eyes met Nick's. "Gay? Oh, this keeps getting better and better. What the hell did you do—sing show tunes to her?"

Dixie said, "That was for his grandmother, but he's great at decorating and picking out accessories." Dixie took Nick's hand. "Anyway, he's a cook—or a chef, if you're feeling fancy about it. Let him go, okay? I'm the one who's making your life miserable and came up here to find you. He's an innocent by-stander out for a walk, a really long walk."

The man sobered and waved his gun toward Nick. "Toss out your weapon."

Dixie shook her head. "You're not getting it. He doesn't have one. He's a cook. *C-o-o-k!* The only weapon he has is a carving knife or a cheese grater. He's got a saucier that's pretty lethal if thrown across the room. Believe me, I did it."

The man waved his gun at Nick again. "Now. And do it slowly. Two fingers. Nothing funny if you want to keep this little lady healthy."

The other men gathered around, and Nick reached into his pocket, and took out his SIG and dropped it on the ground. He watched Dixie's eyes widen to cover her face as parka man said, "Some cook, huh?"

"How'd you get onto me?" Nick asked, trying to figure out where he'd blown his cover.

"We got people in town, too. You and that Wes guy aren't the only ones with secrets."

Nick mentally kicked himself in the ass. "Gracie's ex, Glen. I should have guessed that scum was connected to this operation."

"Bingo. He keeps an eye out for us—we pay him off. He'd snitch out his own mother for a buck. You must have done some number on him, scared the hell out of him. We had to up our payoff or he was leaving town. He overheard you and Wes talking about being agents. Last I heard from old Glen you and your buddies were doing poker at your place and Red here was doing cho—"

"You're…you're an FBI agent?" Dixie interrupted in a squeak that sounded as if she'd just found her voice. She was not taking the news well. What had he expected—hugs and kisses?

"I can explain, Dixie. My plan was to tell you as soon as we caught these guys."

"FBI as in Federal Bureau of Investigation? Not Food, Beverage and Indigestion or something like that? All those feelings I had were right on, and you let me think they weren't? All this time I thought you were a cook and that was it, and you agreed? And just for the record, your plan to get these guys sucks."

Her brow furrowed so deeply her eyebrows met her hairline. Her lips thinned to a slit and she snarled, "You lied to me, Nick Romero. You played me. I was ready to give up my dreams for you."

"You were?" His chest tightened and he felt sick at what he'd just lost.

She looked at parka man. "You don't have to bother shooting him. Don't waste the bullet. I'm going to strangle him with my bare hands."

She threw down the bag of Peeps, spewing them everywhere, and lunged for Nick, yelling, "You creep! You bastard!"

There was a simultaneous sucking in of air as all the men stepped back and Andy—huffing and snorting—trotted in. All eyes cut to him as Jack yelled from the other direction, "Nobody move. This is the sheriff. Drop your weapons and put your hands over your heads."

Nick shoved Dixie behind him to get her the hell out of danger as he pulled the gun from the holster at his ankle and trained it on the smugglers. Swear words polluted the air and guns hit the ground like heavy raindrops. She whispered in his ear from behind, "I don't know how you did that, but it was very cool. But I'm still going to strangle you dead."

He glanced back to her and gave her a crooked grin. "You'll have to wait. Jack needs my help right now and I can't take credit for Andy. I think that was you and the marshmallows. Nice touch."

"FBI? How could I have missed that one? How could I be so stupid?"

"You're not stupid. You trusted me, and I'm sorry

I betrayed that trust, Dixie." He didn't have time for a full apology, but a short one was better than nothing.

"Some investigative reporter I am." Without waiting for his answer, she started walking toward Jack.

Dammit all. He couldn't go after her; he had work to do. Maybe later he'd sit her down and explain all this and hope like mad she understood. Except, that could be a hell of a lot of understanding for someone he'd lied to about so much.

FROM THE DEPOT PORCH, Dixie watched Nick handcuff bad guys and collect weapons, and Andy scarf marshmallows. All things considered, it had been a big night for excitement, except that she'd lost Nick along the way. A black Jeep that she didn't recognize from the Bend approached, adding more headlights to illuminate the area. Two Humvees followed, more tank than truck. Men in black collected the smugglers; others rummaged through the contents of the vans. A box slid from the back, spilling out purses. She remembered the fakes in Nick's room. Guess he needed visual aids to track down the smugglers. Purses weren't his specialty. Well, he sure had lying and deception down pat. In that, the man was a real pro.

With everyone busy, she felt it was a good time to make her escape. She'd had enough of smugglers, the

FBI and especially Nick Romero to last her awhile. Slowly, she backed around the side of the depot—right into Nick's front. She'd know the feel of that torso anywhere and she'd never forget the scent of his soap.

"Leaving so soon?"

She turned. "Home would be nice."

"You have to answer some questions for us, give a statement."

She parked her hands on her hips. "Okay, here's a statement for you, buster. Go to hell."

He raked a hand through his hair. "I understand you're really upset right now and—"

"Upset! This is more than a burned casserole. This is us, you and me. I felt upset the minute FBI got thrown into the mix. Danny going off on a business trip, coming home and making love to me, then serving me with divorce papers, was the lowest of the low. You even got him beat. Congratulations. At least Danny didn't pump me for information, use me to show him around the town and help him fit in. Although you've both succeeded in making me look like a damn fool—I'll give you that."

"It's business, Dixie. FBI business that's important to a lot of people."

"Was making love to me part of that business, too?"

"No, dammit. You got caught in the middle. We got caught in the middle. You mean a lot to me, more than you realize. I made love to you because I care for you. I swear I never meant to hurt you."

"Well, you did, Nick. You really did." She punched his arm because it was a better solution than crying and she refused to cry, especially over a man. "If you want me to answer questions, you'll have to arrest me, because I never intend to talk to you again."

She stepped around him and made for the Camaro, fired it up and headed for Sky Notch. She should tell Maggie and BJ she was okay. She was over her two-hour curfew and they'd be frantic. And she really, really deserved another piece of chocolate cake.

No one stopped her. They probably knew better than to mess with an irate forty-year-old woman who'd just been messed over by one of their own.

She took the back road slow, the night as empty as the feeling in her heart. She should get an SUV...then again she should just sell the Camaro. What good was it if she worked in the city?

She drove up to Maggie's big post-and-beam house and sat in the car for a moment. She was a jerk magnet. If there was a rotten guy within a fifty-mile radius, she found him.

Well, no more. After the lump in her breast, she'd sworn to follow her dreams, live life on her own terms. She had to focus on that, not Nick and how he'd hurt her and how darn much she cared about him. She'd go home tonight, write her "Smuggler Meets Small Western Town and the FBI" story and send it out to the papers. If she got a job offer anywhere—Alaska, Maine, Timbuktu— she'd take it.

She went inside without knocking. Maggie and BJ sat at the kitchen table and stopped talking. Maggie said, "I got to tell you things were a lot simpler around here when you were content being a waitress at the Sage. Where have you been?" They stood and came over to her. "We were frantic, and Jack and Flynn aren't picking up their cells. We were getting ready to head into town or go looking for you or something. What the heck happened to you this time?"

"Nick happened." She sat at the bar in the kitchen, dragged over the cake platter and grabbed a spatula. She scooped a chunk, making sure she got as much icing as possible. This was a big-icing kind of night.

"Well, let's see," BJ said. "You're here eating cake, so you're safe. That's good. And we've ruled out Nick as gay and a smuggler. So, what's next?"

"FBI."

Maggie stared at her for a full minute. "FBI, as he's *in* the FBI."

"Life is full of little surprises. The good news is he and the rest of the band of mighty men captured the smugglers." Dixie smiled at BJ. "Which means the boys and your mom can come home."

"I…I had no idea," Maggie said. "Bet Jack will be shocked Nick is an agent. He didn't have a clue."

"Ha!"

Maggie's eyes drew together and she studied Dixie as she spooned more cake. "Define *ha*."

"Jack knew. Flynn knew. Wes is an agent, too. All part of the band of mighty men. I say we take them out back and beat the hell out of 'em."

BJ stood. "Flynn knew Nick is an agent? *My* Flynn?" She sliced her hand through the air. "Wait just a minute." She massaged her forehead. "They were all there tonight with the smugglers. But…but Nick, Jack, Wes and *my Flynn* stood in that sheriff's office two days ago and—"

"Your Flynn what?" asked Flynn in a too-cheery voice from the hallway. His tone said, *I am in so much do-do, but I'll try to fake my way out of it.* He trooped into the kitchen, followed by Nick and Wes and Jack.

The three women glared at their men.

Chapter Eleven

Maggie nailed Jack with a stare guaranteed to freeze water in ten seconds flat. "*You* stood in that office of yours and told us—" she waved her hand to include BJ and Dixie "—that Nick Romero was a cook, a chef, nothing more. That you had him checked out— I believe those were your exact words. That he and Wes were just who they said they were, period."

Jack swallowed. "He was undercover, Mags."

"Don't you 'Mags' me. You lied to me, to all of us. You didn't have to do that."

"And if who Nick really was had slipped out, he would have been in danger and the whole smuggling operation would have been blown to hell and back."

Flynn folded his arms and said with a disarming smile, "We got the smugglers. Mission accomplished. Everything goes back to normal."

BJ stared back, not disarmed one bit. "If normal is sleeping in your Jeep tonight."

"Jeep?" Flynn unfolded his arms, his smile gone. "That's...unreasonable."

"What's unreasonable is that you didn't trust me to keep your secret."

"You all talk at the Sage," Jack said to Maggie. "What if someone overheard you?"

Nick stepped forward. "This is all my and Wes's fault." He nodded at Jack and Flynn. "They had to keep their mouths shut. The FBI works that way, especially this time, when we were trying to track down smugglers and had no idea where they were. Passing me off as a cook was the simplest plan."

He glanced from BJ to Maggie to Dixie, keeping his eyes on her. She didn't want to look back, but something made her put down the spatula and do it, anyway.

"I apologize for any problems I've caused all of you," he said.

"Me, too," Wes chimed in.

Nick continued. "Lying is part of this job. And with Dixie after the smuggling story and knowing I was FBI, she would have dogged me at every step and put herself in more danger than she was already in."

BJ rounded on Dixie. "Danger? What happened? You were there with the smugglers, weren't you? You didn't arrive after the fact or watch it from afar the way you promised."

"Hey, I found Andy. I threw Peeps out the car

window on the way here so he'd follow." She went to cut more cake, but Maggie snagged the platter.

"What happened tonight?"

"The smugglers showed up," Dixie said. "And Nick came along, and the smugglers recognized him, and that's how I found out what was going on. Andy charged in, followed by Jack, Wes, Flynn and Sam, and they got the drop on the smugglers. Nick shoved me out of the way, so I wasn't in all that much danger." She snagged back the cake.

Maggie cut her attention to Jack. "You saved Dixie?"

"So did I," Flynn said as he pointed to his chest, the hope of not sleeping in the Jeep shining in his eyes. He tried a sheepish smile. "I'm forgiven?"

BJ closed her eyes for a moment. "Maybe." She scooped up Angela and headed for the door. Flynn's grin grew and he gave the thumbs-up sign to the other men as he followed BJ out the door.

"Don't even think you're getting off that easy," Maggie said to Jack. A slow grin brightened her face. "But now that I think about it, there is a way to make it up to me." She hooked her arm through his and headed for the living room. "I've picked out the perfect tux for you. You'll just love it."

He turned and frowned over his shoulder, giving Nick the thumbs-down sign.

"I better tell Gracie what's going on," Wes said.

"My confession's not going to be pretty, but it'll be better if she hears it from me instead of the gossip mill, and even though nothing's official, people will talk." He heaved a deep sigh. "She really does think I'm a photographer." Then he ambled down the hall and left, closing the door after him.

"Well," Nick said. "That just leaves us."

"There is no us." Dixie got a glass of water and studied Nick. So handsome, so strong and brave and determined—and so two-faced.

"I'm sorry. I wish I could think of something else to say, Dixie."

"There's nothing left. You're a terrific FBI agent, and some part of me understands why you did what you did, but I can't live like that, Nick. How can I ever trust you again? I've been down this road before, and I don't like the view. It's too…bumpy."

He sat on a barstool, suddenly exhausted to the core. "I'm retiring, Dixie. That was the plan all along. This is my last job. I'm quitting the bureau and opening a restaurant for real. I thought about opening it in another town, where no one knew me, but I like it here. Whistlers Bend suits me fine…and you're here."

"Do you really have a grandmother?"

He grinned. Using his index finger, he swiped icing from the edge of the cake. "You bet. You'd like her, and she'd like you. You have spunk and you don't let me get away with anything. Everything I told you about her is true except for me giving her the purses and designer stuff for gifts. The guys at the bureau slipped Cher and *Oklahoma!* in the box for fun. Some fun."

Dixie leaned against the counter, suddenly feeling as beat as Nick appeared. "Well, there you go. That's the whole point, isn't it? One part's true. One part's not. What part of you do I trust, Nick? What do I believe in? I'm supposed to think that you can simply quit the bureau and leave your old self behind?"

"Yeah." The sincere expression on his face nearly convinced her…except he was a skilled liar.

"Maybe…maybe not." She turned for the hall and he said, "Since you hate my guts already, there's something else I need to tell you."

She stopped by the stove and glared. "Good grief, now what?"

"That story you're going to write about the smugglers—you can't do it."

"Of course I can. I know what happened. I was there, remember? In fact, it'll be a really good story. I should get a job out of it. Maybe not a terrific reporting job right off, but the story will get me some kind of job."

"No newspaper will pick it up, Dixie. The FBI will deny the whole thing ever happened. We're trying to get to the source of this smuggling, and if we tip the smugglers off, that we're getting close, they'll shut down, move operations somewhere else, and all this is for nothing." He looked her in the eyes. "No one's going to touch your story."

She flattened her palm to her forehead, feeling totally numb. "I should have listened to my mother."

"Never trust a man?"

"Never fall in love. It'll break your heart every time." She turned and left the kitchen. What in the world had she ever done to deserve Nick Romero—or whatever his name really was—in her life? And why in the world did she just tell him she'd fallen in love with him? Stress!

"Wait," Nick said as he caught up with her in the hallway. He stood in front of her so she couldn't leave. "You…you fell in love with me?"

"I was afraid you'd catch that."

"You really thought I wouldn't?"

"I didn't sleep with you on a whim, Nick. I might break in to your house, or go through your things, or have dinner with you on a whim, but not make love to you that way. I fell in love. I'll fall out of it. Forty-year-old women are resilient as hell. Bouncing back is what we do best. I got over Danny. I'll get over you."

"I'm headed for Billings to finish up this case. I'll be back in time for the 5-K run. I said I'd furnish the food and I will. We need to talk. Promise me we'll talk."

"We're talking now. It's not doing either of us one

bit of good." She stepped around him, left and got into her car. Wes might be at Gracie's, and Dixie did not want to rehash the "I'm an FBI agent" scenario again. She headed for the Sage. The late-night crowd would be there now; things would be calm, since the smuggling operation would be kept pretty much a secret. A cup of tea would be good.

She parked in front of the diner, went inside and aimed for the usual table, the *old* usual table. She gazed across the diner to the new table.

Nothing ever stayed the same. BJ had Flynn, Maggie had Jack, and after the 5-K walk/run next week, Dixie had to move on, too.

Chapter Twelve

Dew still clung to the grass as Maggie helped Dixie move the last of the barricades into place. Today Whistlers Bend was a no-vehicle town. Walkers and runners only. For the past three days she and Nick, BJ and Flynn, Maggie and Jack, and Gracie and Wes had worked like mad to take registrations and donations and get volunteers to hand out water and juice at checkpoint.

"Does Nick need help setting up tables for his great pizza bash after the event?" Maggie asked.

"Wes and Gracie are helping him with that."

Maggie stuffed her hands in her jean pockets. "How long do you think you can avoid him, Dixie?"

"I hear Andy's back, horny little devil that he is."

"Forget Andy. We're talking about Nick. He's crazy about you. Everyone in town appreciates that. They've forgiven him for the lies. Heck, he's a town hero. Wes and Gracie are more serious than ever."

"And I'm glad about all that, I really am. BJ will remember to have the runners assemble ahead of the walkers, then participants with strollers and or those pulling their kids in wagons, right?"

Maggie let out a long sign. "You're impossible. You told BJ three times. She went to medical school. She can handle it. Don't worry. Whistle For The Cure will be a big success, not only financially but by making everyone aware. Every woman will get a card explaining self-breast examinations and the importance of mammograms."

"Do we have enough whistles for everyone?"

"The whistles Nick donated, along with the T-shirts and all the food that he spent the past three days cooking. I tell you the aroma coming from Nick's Place has the whole town drooling. You need to understand him, Dixie. The lying was part of the job, not the man."

"Seems to me they're one in the same. How can I separate them?"

"He caught the bad guys, Dix. BJ has her family home with her and Flynn. The FBI is one step nearer to closing down sweatshops that exploit children and use profits for terrorism, prostitution and a lot of other unsavory things."

"He could have told me, Maggie. I'm supposed to trust him when he couldn't trust me?"

"Just forgive him. I've forgiven Jack and BJ's forgiven Flynn. They did what they thought was best to protect us."

"Nick called the shots on this. He could have included me in the loop. I was in on this from the beginning. I found clues, helped him with the whole operation. He told me nothing."

"He had his reasons."

"And I have mine. Lies don't work for me." Dixie checked her watch. "I have to go. It's almost starting time." She smiled. "Let's enjoy the day."

She headed for the Sage and the crowd gathering there. The run's course went from the Purple Sage, around the footpath at the lake, past the docks and old boat rental to the other end of town, then back to the town square. Twice around equaled five miles exactly. Runners would stick to the left, walkers to the right. At noon, Nick would serve pizza and iced tea and lemonade; in the afternoon, there would be homemade ice cream along with the fiddlers from the Cut Loose so everyone could dance.

She remembered dancing with Nick, and the fun they'd had and how they'd made love in the boat rental. She had to get out of Whistlers Bend. Every place she looked she thought of Nick and their time together.

She walked to the front of the crowd and said through the bullhorn, "Welcome, everyone, to the first annual Whistle For The Cure 5-K Run."

The crowd cheered, then started to run or walk. Dixie managed to avoid Nick, even passed on his incredible pizza, which everyone raved about. She ate an apple while getting the trophies ready for presenting. An apple was a pitiful substitute for mushroom pizza. Maybe this was a sign she should start on that diet. Nah, way too extreme.

She had BJ present the trophies to the runners and walkers. Then she introduced three survivors of breast cancer from the Bend, who got the biggest applause of all for winning the biggest battle of all. They'd gotten another chance at life and she had, too; she had to remember that. Dreams were meant to be followed.

Night fell and the town emptied, returning to normal. It took three hours to pick up litter and take down barricades, then Dixie headed to the *Whistle Stop* to write an article about the event. Even old Eversole couldn't give her grief on putting this news on the front page, complete with the pictures Wes took. Whistle For The Cure was simply too big a success.

Everyone was happy, except for her. She wanted Nick. As much as she tried to force him out of her thoughts and throw herself into the day's activities, he had been there, running around in her head all day, driving her nuts, making her sad. But what could she do? Say, *Oh, Nick darling, I forgive you and will trust you for the rest of my life.*

She could say that, but she wouldn't mean it. He'd lied a lot and it mattered.

When she left the *Whistle Stop* office, it was nearly 2:00 a.m. She walked the deserted streets from the office to Gracie's. A breeze ruffled the deciduous trees, which would soon be turning gold and red, the pines waiting for the snows sure to follow.

Kate and Cameron were spending the night at BJ's to celebrate Drew's and Pete's return, leaving Gracie alone. But Wes would not be spending the night with her. Gracie and Wes were courting now, but no casual sex for the mother of two kids. She and Wes had decided it just wasn't right.

Dixie went up the front walk to her sister's. A dog barked in the distance, but other than that her foot-steps were the only sound. She turned the knob to let herself in, except the door was locked. That was a good thing, meaning Gracie had taken Nick's warn-ing about Glen seriously. But it was also bad, because Dixie had forgotten the darn key.

Sleeping on the porch had definite appeal because she was so tired, but a bed had more. Just a few more steps, she encouraged herself, as she went around to the basement door. She found the key under the third flowerpot on the left and let herself in.

The scent of fresh paint washed over her as she flipped on the overhead lights illuminating the Hair Flair. Sinks, chairs, dryers were in place, supplies stood piled on the stairs, waiting for the new cabinets scheduled for delivery tomorrow— And Glen was staring right at her. Fatigue vanished. Apprehension settled in as he growled, "What the hell are you doing down here?"

"Why do you have a gasoline can in your... Holy cow!"

"Yeah." His lips curled in a sour smile. "Holy cow." He pulled a gun from his waistband.

"Does everyone own a gun these days? I hate guns," Dixie said.

"You should have stayed with your boyfriend tonight, because I'm going to burn this place to the ground and get the insurance money. The kids are gone, Gracie's upstairs and I sure don't give a crap about her or you."

Great. Now what? "Your name's not on the deed anymore, Glen. Forget this. Go crawl back under a rock and leave Gracie and the kids alone."

"You think you're so damn smart. The insurance money will go to the kids, and I get the kids because I'm their papa. Knowing Gracie, she's probably got a nice life insurance policy. And you showing up is a real good thing, now that I think about it. I bet old Gracie left the kids to you, so if I can get you out of the picture along with her, the kids and money are mine without any legal problems."

"Why are you doing this?"

"Hell, why do you think? I need money. My supply dried up. Word has it your boyfriend and that Wes guy had something to do with bringing down the smugglers and costing me a real sweet job with them."

From the corner of her eye, Dixie caught sight of Gracie creeping down the steps, carefully tiptoeing around the supply boxes. Okay, now what? Keep Glen's attention and give Gracie time to concoct some great idea, whatever that was.

"The kids are upstairs, Glen," Dixie ventured, hoping that would change his mind or just keep his attention on her. "Kate had a sore throat."

Gracie took another step down and Dixie added in a rush, "And Gracie isn't alone. Wes is with her right now."

"Gracie wouldn't do that with the kids here. She's all about doing things right. You're lying through your teeth."

"Trust me. Wes is here and Nick is on his way. We're all going to have a midnight snack." How pathetic an excuse!

"Well, ain't that special." Glen gave a cynical laugh that said he wasn't buying this explanation for one minute. Gracie tried the next stair, except this one creaked. Gracie was the good daughter; she'd never learned to walk on the edges!

Glen spun around as Gracie snapped up a can of hairspray, yanked off the lid and zapped Glen right between the eyes before he could figure out what in the world she was doing.

He yowled in pain, dropped the gun to the new linoleum—hopefully, it didn't make a dent—then grabbed his face as Dixie charged, capturing him in a full-body lunge, sending them both to the floor. Least he was underneath her and cushioned the impact. Glen was good for something after all!

"You're killing me. You're killing me," Glen yelled. He swore and fought as Dixie sat on his butt and wrestled one arm back. Gracie tripped down the last step, sending boxes everywhere. She plopped down next to Dixie and wrangled back Glen's other arm.

"Get off me!" Glen swore again, and Dixie grabbed a blow-dryer from the overturned box, wrapped the cord around one wrist, then the other, and pulled tight.

Dixie stared at her sister. "I knew you were a natural at this salon stuff. Nice shot with the hairspray."

"I can't breathe," Glen moaned.

Gracie laughed. "I don't care." She said to Dixie, "Sister power. Better than ever." They exchanged high-fives. "Guess we should call Jack."

"Maybe Wes and Nick. Glen is part of the smuggling operation. He might have some information the FBI can use." She poked Glen in the ribs and he grunted. "Glen here has been a really big pain for a really long time, and the creep was going to barbecue us tonight. He deserves jail and all its amenities, such as the friends he'll meet there."

Dixie got up, rummaged through the boxes on the steps and held up a little purple bottle. "You should show Glen here how really good you are with hair care," she said to Gracie. "I think you should streak his hair blond. He'll be so appealing to all his new friends in jail."

Glen wiggled, nearly upending Gracie. "You can't do this to me. I'll be… Everyone will think I'm… You know what will happen to me in jail if I go there looking like that!"

Gracie sighed. "We can't dye his hair, Dixie, unless we give him a manicure, too. Flamingo Pink. Do his toenails to match. I have some perfume samples. His new roommates will be so impressed. I have a new depilatory. We could test it out on his legs. Smooth-leg Glen could be his new name."

"You can't do this," Glen wailed. "I'm sorry, okay? I should never have tried to burn you out. Don't shave my legs! Don't do any of this."

Dixie dumped the purple liquid into a bowl and found a streaking brush, then handed it to Gracie as she straddled Glen's back. "When we get done with you, Glen, you're going to be so lovely."

NICK PRIED OPEN ONE EYE, grabbed the cell phone from the nightstand and grumbled, "It better be good."

"It is."

"Dixie?" He hadn't talked to her since their parting at the ranch. Oh, there'd been the monosyllabic exchanges over the 5-K run, but that was all. "What's up?" he asked as he parked himself on the edge of his bed, feeling himself come awake instantly.

She said she had a hair dryer he might be interested in and he should bring Wes, that it was important and she and Gracie were sitting on something big and beautiful. She disconnected. "What the hell?"

But if Dixie was talking to him, he was listening. In the past two weeks, he'd tried everything to get her to listen to him. He'd had flowers and doughnuts delivered to her every morning, cookies at night, casseroles of linguine, lasagna and ziti. But not a word of acknowledgment till now.

He shrugged on his clothes and met up with Wes as he ambled up Gracie's walk. "What's going on?" Nick asked.

"Beats the hell out of me. Gracie said to bring my camera." The light was on in the new salon, so they aimed for that. A new red canvas awning sporting Hair Flair in gold letters covered the doorway, with pots of flowers on either side. "Hi," said Dixie as he and Wes entered. She and Gracie were sitting on someone. She gave a little finger wave. "We have a present for you."

She got up, then Gracie did. Nick stared. "Glen? I think. What happened to his hair?"

"Don't let them sit on me any more, man. My functionality as a male has been seriously compromised and my eyelashes are stiff as a board. They shaved my freaking legs. Isn't there a law or something?"

Wes nudged the gas can. "I take it this isn't the newest thing in hair care."

Gracie sobered. "It could have been bad. But now he's going to jail, and Dixie and I got him all gussied up for the occasion. Besides a new hairdo, he's got a new manicure and pedicure and he's smelling oh, so sweet. He's all ready for the jail in Billings."

Nick and Wes laughed and Glen barked, "I have rights, dammit, rights."

Wes aimed his camera. "I'll get some shots of the gas can. Send some guys down to take prints from the doors. You need to give a statement," he said to Gracie. "Mind coming into Billings? Can't wait to hear the whole story." He nodded to Nick. "He can transport Glen so he won't bother you anymore."

"I'll stay here and get the kids in the morning, which isn't all that far off," Dixie said.

Gracie purred to Wes, "I'll change and be right back. Maybe you should help me pick out what to wear."

Wes's cheeks reddened to the color of Gracie's new awning. "I...I can do that."

They left, and Nick sat in one of the swivel styling chairs and leaned back. "Didn't have enough action for one day? Had to scare up more?"

"This was so not my doing, except I helped with the dye job."

Her eyes sparkled. She was made to be a reporter. She loved the action and being in on everything. How could he deny her that? "I found Glen trying to collect fire and life insurance all at one time," she said. "I distracted him while Gracie shot him with Volumizing with Extra Hold. We tied him up, then glamorized him."

Nick chuckled. "Takedown Dixie-style."

"And Gracie's." She smiled, but there was a glint of something serious in her eyes. "There's more. You'll be interested in how I distracted Glen. I lied my butt off. I told Glen so many fibs I'm surprised my tongue didn't fall out of my mouth. Funny how that happened."

"I don't think any of this is funny at all," Glen mumbled.

Nick glared at Glen, who then added, "All right, all right. I'll shut up."

Dixie continued. "I had to save my sister and lying seemed like a very small price to pay." She let out a big breath. "Besides, it's not like I haven't lied before. Truth be told, I'm probably the queen of lying. I'm sorry I've given you such a hard time lately. It's just that—"

"You were hurt and this was personal," Nick said, suddenly feeling closer to Dixie Carmichael than ever. "Does this mean we—you and me—have a chance?"

"I'm going to drive to Denver, maybe get something at the *Post,* maybe not. I have to try, Nick. You understand that. Heard you're putting the finishing touches on the restaurant."

"I'm going to cater Jack and Maggie's wedding."

He stood as Gracie and Wes returned. Dixie went for the stairs. He watched her go. He did a lot of that lately. And he hated it. He had his dream; she had hers. He just didn't know how to get the two together.

By the next afternoon he still didn't have a clue, and it wasn't for a lack of trying. All the way to Billings and back.

He answered a knock at the front door, signed for another shipment of pasta dishes he'd ordered as Dixie came toward him, waving a letter, totally happy. Damn, he liked seeing her that way—radiant, full of life, ready for fun. He'd miss that. *He'd miss her.*

"What's got you in such a good mood?" he asked as she entered the restaurant.

She gazed around. "Wow! This place is fabulous. I like the fountain in the middle and the trellis effect overhead. Cozy and not stuffy."

"That's what I was aiming for." Others had stopped and complimented him on the restaurant, but none of those compliments mattered as much as Dixie's. "So, what's with the letter? Good news?"

"I got this from the *Boston Globe.* Seems they

picked up that panning article I did on you and liked it. They're interested in seeing more articles. Just freelance, of course. Still… You're not looking all that surprised."

That was because he was taking in every wonderful inch of Dixie Carmichael. Totally enjoying her and not paying that much attention to what she was saying. Besides, he already knew. "Hey, I'm surprised all to hell. So, tell me more."

She gave him the squinty-eyed stare. "You did this." She waved the letter in the air. "You got the *Globe* interested in me."

"Dixie, I'm with—or *was* with—the FBI."

"With newspaper connections. You admitted that when you told me the papers wouldn't pick up my smuggling story and here's the *Globe* picking up another story of mine. All that picking up seems a little too coincidental. And the *Globe* is in Boston. You were raised in Boston. I may not be an FBI agent, but I can put that together easy enough."

"I sent a guy I grew up with the article. But he wouldn't have bought it if he hadn't liked what he read. That's the truth. You're not going to turn his offer down, are you? It's a good opportunity, exactly what you want. What you deserve." *And what he didn't want at all. But…*

A grin slid across her face. "I guess I should say thanks. I won't let you down."

She kissed him, making him happier and sadder than he'd ever been in his life. He'd helped her realize her dream, but she was leaving and Boston was far away. "Let me fix you a celebration dinner."

Even though she still smiled, her eyes clouded with sadness. "I...can't. I haven't told BJ or Maggie about the letter and I'm meeting them at the Sage—" she checked her watch "—right now and I have to pack and tie up loose ends and... Well, you get the picture." She swallowed. "Besides, I really suck at goodbyes."

His heart physically ached. He hadn't thought her going would be this painful. He forced a grin. "If you've never driven in Boston, maybe you should fly in."

He was just filling time, finding anything to talk about. He couldn't give her up, not yet.

"I've considered that, but the Camaro is who I am and it would be like leaving everything behind." Her voice hitched and she gazed at him. "I can't leave everything."

Leaving. Damn, he hated that word. Maybe because that was what the women in his life did. For whatever reason, they left him. "Well then, Dixie Carmichael, have a safe trip. I'll miss you."

MORNING CROWD filled the tables at the Sage as Maggie fidgeted in the booth. "I can't believe this is our last breakfast together." She nodded to Dixie's car, which sat parked on the street. "How'd you fit all your stuff in a Camaro?"

BJ drummed her fingers on the tabletop. "You have maps and your AAA card and your cell's charged and—"

Dixie stilled BJ's fingers and continued to hold her hand. "I'll be okay. And I'll be back for Maggie's wedding."

"I bet you'll be too busy or too caught up in your new life," Maggie huffed.

She sounded as sad as Dixie felt. "I'd never be that busy," she said. "I'll be back."

Maggie nodded at the new waitress as she refilled coffee cups, served up breakfast and took orders. "She's okay, but she's not you."

Dixie needed every ounce of self-control not to jump up and help. Her waitress days were over, she reminded herself. "She'll be fine. Waitressing takes a little getting used to, and for the customers to get used to her."

"Have you seen Nick?"

"Day before yesterday. We said goodbye then."

"Well then," Maggie said as she studied her fingernails, trying to look nonchalant but failing miserably. "I suppose you don't know about the auction." She pulled a yellow paper from her purse and skidded it across the table to Dixie. "My, my, I wonder what it's all about."

Dixie read the flyer, feeling her head start to throb.

"He's selling off the restaurant? Why would he do such a thing?"

BJ took her hand. "You're asking the wrong person, Dix, and I so think you should ask the right one."

Dixie checked her watch. "The auction's starting in fifteen minutes. This makes no sense." She felt her brain fog. "What is that man doing now? Nick's Place is his dream. He quit the FBI for it. He was ready to open, just waiting on the white rattan tables and chairs he'd ordered."

Maggie stirred her coffee. "Guess it isn't as big a dream as he thought. Maybe he has other dreams." She put down her spoon and said to BJ, "Think I'll walk on over to the auction. What about you?"

BJ stood. "Good idea." She gazed down at Dixie. "Coming? Or going?"

"If this is something you two cooked up, I'll—"

"No way." Maggie dropped enough money for the coffee and a tip on the table. "Whatever Nick has planned is all his own doing and I didn't know anything about it till this morning, when I got this flyer taped to my mailbox. Aren't you dying of curiosity? I sure am. Maybe you should ask Nick. At least show up and find out."

BJ smiled too sweetly. "'Course we can write you all about it. Tell you want happened."

"You? Write? Either of you? I'll be dead and in my grave before that happens."

BJ added her money to Maggie's. "Probably." She put Angela in the stroller and followed Maggie out of the Sage.

A pout pulled Dixie's lips together. They didn't even see her off, wave from the sidewalk, throw rose petals in her wake, and they'd left a bigger tip for the new gal than they'd ever left for her.

What was going on? She could drive out of Whistlers Bend and get on with her life…though she'd probably combust from a terminal case of curiosity before she crossed the state line.

Five minutes, that was all it would take to stop by, see what was going on, satisfy her insatiable nosiness, and then she could leave town in peace.

Dixie added her money to the others and walked up the street to Nick's Place. A crowd was already spilling out of the restaurant onto the sidewalk. She walked faster and started elbowing her way in as people gave her dirty looks, but suddenly she didn't care about them—only about Nick.

She got as close as she could, till the throng became too tightly packed for her to press on. The old ladder he'd been on that first day she and Nick met lay propped against the wall. She climbed up the first two rungs. Nick had piled boxes of his new dishes on the table beside boxes of glassware beside boxes marked table linens. Other boxes stood against the wall; unassembled bistro tables lay in a heap in the corner.

She waved her hand to get his attention, and when his eyes focused on her, he smiled hugely, his eyes bright and filled with happiness, making her feel happy she hadn't left. He wedged himself through the noisy crowd till he reached her. "What is this all about?" she asked.

"I'm selling out, Dixie." He stepped up onto the ladder beside her and kissed her full on the lips right there in front of half the population of Whistlers Bend. "I'm going to Boston with you." The crowd quieted, suddenly captivated by the conversation, and she couldn't blame them—she was pretty captivated, too.

"What are you talking about?" She gestured at the restaurant. "This is what you want. You told me so. Everyone in town will swear to that."

He kissed her again, taking her breath away. "You're what I want." The crowd went dead quiet, the female half—and maybe some of the males—letting out an audible sigh of appreciation. He continued. "I'm auctioning the restaurant stuff off and then selling the building to Wes for his photo studio."

She grabbed his arms. "Nick, you hate big cities. This is a bad idea."

"I'll get a job in one of the restaurants there. Boston has tons of great restaurants. I can find my way around. It's where I grew up. I got this covered, Dixie. I want us to have a chance together, and that's not going to happen if I'm here and you're in Boston. I've got to be in Boston, too, with you. I finally figured out what was wrong in my life. Women have always left me and I hated that. Then I realized it wasn't their leaving me that was the problem, but my not going after them. I'm going after you, Dixie. I want to be with you."

A lady in the back said that was the most romantic thing she'd ever heard, and the crowd nodded in agreement, a few people dabbed moist eyes. Nick made his way back to the auctioning table. He swung a hammer against a chunk of wood. "The first things on the auction block are the dishes." He held up a pasta plate. "Basket-weave pattern, good quality, dishwasher and microwave safe."

Dixie remembered the first time he'd cooked for her and he'd told her about his plans for Nick's and…

"I'll take them all," Dixie blurted. "Whatever you paid for them."

Every eye focused on her, and Nick said, "Dixie? What will you do with all that china? You're moving to Boston."

"I'll make a lot of friends." She scribbled a check and passed it through the crowd making its way up to Nick.

He studied it, shook his head, then held up a wineglass. The ones with bubbles blown into the glass, which Nick had liked more than the cheaper glasses. Dixie yelled, "I'll take them all…to go with the china." He gave her an incredulous look and she wrote out another check and passed it forward.

"The next items," Nick said, "are the tablecloths and napkins." He held up one tablecloth. "The color is—"

"Italian Sunset," Dixie said. "The same color as the Roman shades on order for the windows. A great color. I'll take them. And I'll take the fountain and the bistro tables." His eyes met hers, and she remembered when he'd shown her a picture of what he'd had in mind. She wrote another check.

Nick shook his head. "Well, that brings us to the stove and—"

"I'll take it." How could she let someone have the stove he loved so much? "And the refrigerator." She made out yet her check.

"That's all I have. Except—" his eyes met hers across the crowd "—the chef."

"He's kind and thoughtful and brave and fun and a darn good dancer," Maggie blurted. "And your life without Nick in it will suck."

"All those things are true," Dixie said. Everyone was pin-drop quiet. "I'd love to take the chef."

He laughed and came to her and scooped her into his arms. "Sold," he said. The crowd cheered and Nick kissed her as she wrapped her arms around his strong neck. She loved him with all her heart, every inch of him.

Nick set her down and the crowd slowly filed out

of the restaurant, promising to return when the tables got delivered and Nick's Place opened for business. Nick closed the door. "You didn't have to do any of this, you realize. I really meant it when I said I was selling out to follow you to Boston. It wasn't a trick."

"But now you don't have to."

He picked up the checks she'd written him and put them in her hand. "I don't need these. All I want is you."

"Then we'll be partners in Nick's Place. I'm a great waitress." She smiled. "And I wouldn't be happy in Boston without you. You make me so happy, Nick, happier than any newspaper job ever could."

He kissed her forehead, his lips on her skin a touch of heaven. "I've got some business to take care of. Me staying here wasn't in my plans."

"You have to tell Wes the place isn't for sale?"

"But there's another place. I'll be right back, okay?"

"I can come with you."

"You unpack our dishes and glasses."

And she did, then put together one of the bistro tables. She was happy, really happy. She and Nick would be working together as partners.

The front door opened and Nick came in. She asked, "Did you get Wes a place for his studio?"

"Above the *Whistle Stop,* and he has a job on the newspaper."

Dixie felt her eyes bulge. "Eversole agreed to hire

on Wes? He's such a skinflint I never would have imagined he'd do such a thing."

"I have powers of persuasion with the editor—at least, I hope so." He handed her an official-looking paper. "Bill of sale for the *Whistle Stop.* I bought it from Eversole for you. I know it's not the *Boston Globe,* but it's all yours, to make whatever you want of it. You gave me my dream, Dixie, the restaurant. I had every intention of following you to Boston. I wanted to give you your dream, at least partly."

She studied the paper in her hand. "You did this for me? How did you get that geezer to sell?"

"Well, I had all these checks and Eversole likes mining a lot more than running a newspaper. He's always wanted to try his hand at finding gold. And I think dinner every week was mentioned." Nick laughed. "You want me to live the life I want and I want that for you with all my heart. I love you, Dixie Carmichael."

He fished in his pocket and pulled out a filigree ring with an emerald-and-diamond setting. "This has been in the Romero family forever, and that's what I want you to be. Celest sent it to me when I told her I was planning to marry you if you'd have me. I love you, Dixie."

She threw her arms around his neck. "I love you, Nick, and I'll marry you. You are my dream, the happiness I've always wanted."

Epilogue

Dixie pointed out the upstairs window of Maggie's house to the gleaming white tent on the lawn of Sky Notch. "I can't believe we invited all these people to our wedding. What were we thinking?"

"*Weddings,*" Maggie corrected. "And will you quit fidgeting, so I can fasten these pearls around your neck?"

BJ pinned up a wayward strand of Maggie's hair that had had the audacity to come loose. "We've all lived here forever and sat at that table at the Sage for years, hashing out our lives. It only seemed right that our friends and neighbors would help us celebrate today."

Dixie laughed. "They've listened to us grouse and complain enough."

"I still can't believe Nick catered his own wedding and cooked days," BJ said.

"I can't believe we all found wedding dresses we like," Maggie said.

"I think we were motivated," Dixie said, then added, "things sure have changed for us in the past three months since we turned the big 4-0." She held out her hands to her two lifelong friends and they each took one. "Okay, here we go. Are we all ready?"

Their gazes met and Maggie smiled. "We each have our own lives, doing what we want to do, and we have wonderful men to share our lives with. We are incredibly lucky women."

Dixie grinned. "We're forty and we are so fabulous."

BJ laughed and nodded. "And we're late." She led the way down the steps. They crossed the lawn, the harp and violin music drifting from the tent as a breeze tangled in the trees.

When they got to the entrance to the tent, Maggie nodded at the musicians and the sound of the "Wedding March" filled the space. She started down the aisle, followed by BJ, then Dixie. Jack, Flynn and Nick were waiting, incredibly dashing in dark suits.

The three couples stood before the judge. "Friends," she said, "we are gathered here today to join this man and this woman." She nodded at Maggie and Jack. "And this man and this woman." She nodded at Dixie and Nick. "And affirm the joining of this man and this woman." She nodded at BJ and Flynn. "In holy matrimony."

HARLEQUIN®

AMERICAN *Romance*®

Fatherhood

Fatherhood: what really defines a man.

It's the one thing all women admire in a man—
a willingness to be responsible for a child and
to care for that child with tenderness and love.

Daddy Lessons
by Victoria Chancellor
(January 2006)

Kate Wooten and her son are starting over in
Ranger Springs, Texas. So is Luke Simon, a former
bachelor who needs Kate's help to turn him into a
good father in just two short weeks....

Sugartown
by Leandra Logan
(March 2006)

Sheriff Colby Evans stays away from serious
relationships because of his son. But he can't seem
to keep away from Sugartown's newest resident,
Tina Mills, who's got young Jerod's
seal of approval!

Available wherever Harlequin books are sold.

eHARLEQUIN.com

The Ultimate Destination for Women's Fiction

For **FREE online reading,** visit
www.eHarlequin.com now and enjoy:

Online Reads
Read **Daily** and **Weekly** chapters from
our Internet-exclusive stories by your
favorite authors.

Interactive Novels
Cast your vote to help decide how these
stories unfold...then stay tuned!

Quick Reads
For shorter romantic reads, try our
collection of Poems, Toasts, & More!

Online Read Library
Miss one of our online reads?
Come here to catch up!

Reading Groups
Discuss, share and rave with other
community members!

For great reading online,
visit www.eHarlequin.com today!

INTONL04R

HARLEQUIN®

AMERICAN *Romance*®

US MARSHALS
BORN AND BRED

MARRYING THE MARSHAL

Laura Marie Altom

U.S. Marshal Caleb Logue's new assignment is protecting the eight-year-old son he didn't know he had. Allie Hayworth wouldn't marry him nine years ago—claiming a lawman husband could make for an early widowhood—but she's darn well going to marry him now!

(HAR #1099)
On sale January 2006

Available wherever Harlequin books are sold.

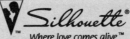

If you enjoyed what you just read,
then we've got an offer you can't resist!

Take 2 bestselling love stories FREE!

Plus get a FREE surprise gift!

Clip this page and mail it to Harlequin Reader Service®

IN U.S.A.	**IN CANADA**
3010 Walden Ave.	P.O. Box 609
P.O. Box 1867	Fort Erie, Ontario
Buffalo, N.Y. 14240-1867	L2A 5X3

YES! Please send me 2 free Harlequin American Romance® novels and my free surprise gift. After receiving them, if I don't wish to receive anymore, I can return the shipping statement marked cancel. If I don't cancel, I will receive 4 brand-new novels every month, before they're available in stores! In the U.S.A., bill me at the bargain price of $4.24 plus 25¢ shipping & handling per book and applicable sales tax, if any*. In Canada, bill me at the bargain price of $4.99 plus 25¢ shipping & handling per book and applicable taxes**. That's the complete price and a savings of at least 10% off the cover prices—what a great deal! I understand that accepting the 2 free books and gift places me under no obligation ever to buy any books. I can always return a shipment and cancel at any time. Even if I never buy another book from Harlequin, the 2 free books and gift are mine to keep forever.

154 HDN DZ7S
354 HDN DZ7T

Name	(PLEASE PRINT)	
Address	Apt.#	
City	State/Prov.	Zip/Postal Code

Not valid to current Harlequin American Romance® subscribers.

Want to try two free books from another series?
Call 1-800-873-8635 or visit www.morefreebooks.com.

* Terms and prices subject to change without notice. Sales tax applicable in N.Y.
** Canadian residents will be charged applicable provincial taxes and GST.
   All orders subject to approval. Offer limited to one per household.
   ® are registered trademarks owned and used by the trademark owner and or its licensee.

AMER04R   ©2004 Harlequin Enterprises Limited